Reckoning at Redemption

RAY NOLAN

A Black Horse Western

ROBERT HALE · LONDON

© Ray Nolan 2001
First published in Great Britain 2001

ISBN 0 7090 6869 7

Robert Hale Limited
Clerkenwell House
Clerkenwell Green
London EC1R 0HT

Typeset by
Derek Doyle & Associates, Liverpool.
Printed and bound in Great Britain by
Antony Rowe Limited, Wiltshire

ONE

He knew he was going to die, and the realization terrified him.

He'd seen others die, naturally and violently, but until now he'd spared no more than a passing thought to his own death and how it might come.

Now, here in these cursed hills, wind tearing at his wet, inadequate clothing, he knew his time was fast creeping up on him.

More than an hour ago the pounding rain had finally petered out giving way to a fierce and biting wind suddenly blasting its way into existence, stinging through his numbed flesh, cutting to the marrow of his bones.

Like his feet encased in scuffed and muddy bench-made boots, his gloved hands were little more than freezing chunks of meat. Each breath swallowed was like an icicle tearing at his lungs.

Desperately he wanted to rest, to give way to the drowsiness clawing at him, but to do so would be easy surrender to the inevitable. His only hope of survival was to keep moving, even though he had little idea of where the rough and narrow trail he followed would take him.

The toe of his boot hooked a rain-exposed root and sent him sprawling. For what seemed a long time he lay in the mud, sobbing in frustration, cursing the circumstances that had driven him to where he was, damning the fool horse for losing its footing, almost taking him with it over the edge of the high and narrow pass.

A whimpering cry of self-pity scraped out of his throat when he shoved up on to his elbows. It was no use. It was stupid to believe that if he could make it through this night he'd be able to make it all the way. Even if he found shelter he was without blankets or food, without so much as dry matches to try and start a fire – with nothing but the sodden and muddy clothes clinging to his body. And the holstered gun dragging heavily against his thigh.

His mouth opened to curse the fates, the rotten luck that had forced him into this pocket of hell, but no sound came. Instead he stiffened, the chattering of his teeth stilled.

Anxious, narrowed eyes raked the almost impenetrable darkness, and found nothing. A sob of utter futility dragged painfully up from his chest, froze in his throat, and turned into a soft, almost insane, cry of relief.

It hadn't been his imagination! There it was again! On higher ground, some distance ahead, a small red glow winking briefly at him.

Absolutely motionless he stared, again found the tiny flickering before once more it was blotted up by the dark.

In his ears was the muffled rattle of half-crazed laughter when he made it to his feet, a newborn strength stirring within him. Clumsily he pushed forward, eyes fastened firmly on the spot where he'd sighted the small, flickering flames of what had to be someone's camp-fire.

He came first upon the horses, not seeing them until hearing an uneasy nicker, the nervous stirring of hoofs. It brought him up short, eyes straining against the dark. There were three of them, tethered in a small clearing where brush and high rock formations offered protection against the elements. Even the howl of the wind was muffled.

Three horses . . . three riders. Until then he'd simply assumed they'd be range men who'd offer food and an opportunity to dry out at their fire. And if they were? And headed to where he had come from. . . ? Unconsciously he shook his head. That was the very last place he wanted to be.

Another sobering thought struck home. What if those whose fire he approached were the kind not to welcome unbidden entry into their camp? Especially by someone anxious to continue in the direction he was presently headed – someone in desperate need of a mount but with nothing to offer by way of payment or trade.

With no recollection of reaching for it, he found his gun in his hand, a coldness that had no connection with the weather taking a grip on his spine. *Would riders with nothing to hide or fear make camp here when the saloons, hotels and restaurants of Astoria were only hours away?*

From the other side of the brush, through which could be seen small, dancing flames, he sensed rather than heard movement. Then, giving him no time to consider his next move, a blacker smudge seemed to appear against the darkness not far from where he crouched. He felt eyes upon him, heard the quiet scrape of boot leather, the rustle of cloth. . . .

His finger tightened around the trigger of the gun he fisted.

Above the almost deafening blasts of three rapid shots he could hear a voice shouting a name and the whinny of horses tugging against picket lines as they reared away from the racket of gunfire.

All of this heard within split seconds, and in only the vaguest way, for already he was scrambling around the brush that screened the camp.

Close to the fire another figure was swiftly rising from his blankets, tall and bearded, clawing loose a gun from a belt and holster scooped up from the ground.

Twice more he fired, saw the man stagger back under the leaden impact slowly twist and crumble.

He let out his breath, but it was a while before his trembling hand could lower the smoking weapon.

With the luxury of food under his belt, warmth seeping slowly back into his body, he hunkered before the fire, sipping still more of the scalding coffee. Both mind and body screamed for sleep, but fear of what might be dogging his trail overcame the temptation to succumb to their demands. Reaching for another piece of the wood gathered by those whose camp he'd invaded, he tossed it into the flames which were already stretched two feet high.

Yet again his eyes roved the camp. They'd found a good spot, those two; a brush-screened hollow gouged into the side of the cliff that provided just about total protection against both wind and rain.

He'd been mistaken about the horses representing three riders. One had been used to pack their gear, of which there was a fair amount. He'd also been wrong about the old man who'd come only to check the animals. But with more important things to think about he wasted no time in shoving aside all memory of the incident.

He stood up. Already he'd delayed too long. The weather showed signs of breaking and if anyone was behind him they'd be getting ready to move again. It was time to do the same. Tossing aside the tin cup, he turned to where the horses were picketed and hesitated.

Money. He needed money.

He moved over to the second man he'd shot. He lay as he'd fallen, awkwardly on his side. From what showed of his bearded face, he'd been the younger of the pair.

Using a foot he rolled the body on to its back, letting loose a startled and frightened yelp at the sound of a soft groan.

His finger was already squeezing when, in the light from the fire, he saw the gleam of blood soaking the man's shirt-front. He let the gun sag. No point in wasting a bullet on someone already banging at death's door.

Sliding the Colt back between leather, getting ready to search the pockets of the man at his feet, his gaze paused at where the shirt had pulled free from worn and patched jeans. . . .

TWO

Rourke paused outside the livery barn, reaching for his tobacco while giving the sky's thickening grey another questioning glance. Yesterday it had been the same, but the rain continued to hold back.

With a cigarette built he touched a match flame to the tip, his gaze sliding along the wide street pausing briefly at the Wells Fargo office where the afternoon stage, its passengers already debarked, waited for a fresh team to be hitched up.

Nearing the end of the second block, his pace slowed. On the other side of the alley, in front of the general store, a grizzled old character, hands dug deep into the pockets of a hand-me-down coat that made him look even skinnier, was staring curiously into the back of a loaded buckboard. Sweat-stained and without shape, his hat looked as if it had gone through the war twice.

Rourke reached the end of the sidewalk just as a heavy figure emerged from the store. Two nights ago he'd seen him in the Phoenix, laughing and whooping it up with a couple of other punchers leaned against the long bar. In him now there was no trace of that humour.

The old-timer's head jerked up, hands wrenching free from the coat pockets. A startled animal-like sound scratched from his gap-toothed mouth. He started to turn, to run, but the man was already upon him, grabbing, bundling up the front of his shirt.

'Damnit, dummy, I told you before – keep away!' He shook the oldster roughly, jerking loose another whimpering cry of fear. 'This's the last time I tell you!' His free hand slashed across the gaunt, grey-stubbled face. 'The last time! Savvy?'

'Charley Noonan!' a female voice shouted from somewhere on the other sidewalk. 'Take your hands off him!'

In the midst of her demand there came a ripping sound when suddenly the old man yanked himself loose, leaving the stocky number holding nothing but part of a torn shirt. With another of those peculiar cries, he aimed a kick at the heavier man's shin before dodging around the buckboard, reaching the alley at the same time as Rourke chose to cross it.

He moved fast, nimbly avoiding a collision, but right behind him was the man he'd kicked – and his path led hard into Rourke. The impact jarred him back on to his heels. He staggered, regained his balance, swore, and moved to thrust aside the obstacle.

Rourke brushed his arm away. 'Careful!'

He was of only average height the one glaring up at Rourke, with shoulders narrower than his thick middle. A heavy moustache completely covered a long upper lip, and in eyes circled by puffy folds of flesh, fire raged.

'Get out of my damn way!' he bellowed. 'I'm gonna kill that crazy, thievin' old bastard!'

Again he tried to shove the taller man out of his

way. Then, realizing he was not about to budge, balled up a fist and swung with everything he had. Rourke stepped easily to the left, driving his own fist into the man's protruding belly, surprised to find it a lot harder than it looked. The blow drove the squat one backwards, jarring him hard against the low edge of the sidewalk. For a wild moment he struggled to stay upright, but his legs refused to co-operate, dropping his broad rump solidly on to the planks.

This time his curse came like a blast from a desert storm. He grabbed for his gun, almost had it free, then went very still, staring at the Colt pointing down at his chest.

From across the street a man wearing a buckskin vest, brown corduroy trousers and highly polished boots had been watching the action with amusement. But seeing Charley Noonan go down, the smirking smile slid from his smoothly shaven face. Thumbs unhooked themselves from his belt and in long strides sheriff's deputy Manny Ebson started for the alley.

By the time he got there Noonan was back on his feet, the other's gun returned to its holster.

'You all right Charley?'

Noonan jerked angrily at his hat-brim, grunted something unintelligible, and turned back to the waiting wagon.

The deputy's eyes ran slowly over Rourke's faded Levis and worn brush-jacket, dismissing him as just another rider of little consequence. 'Mister,' he said slowly, 'in this town we don't tol'rate gunplay on our streets. You're under arrest.'

'Let it go, Manny,' Noonan called down from the buckboard seat. 'Let it go,' he repeated, and this time an ominous note tinged his words. Next moment wheels were crunching through the dust of the street.

Rourke shrugged. 'Guess that takes care of it.' From the corner of his vision he caught sight of the old man huddled against a wall down at the far end of the alley, watching.

'The hell it does,' Ebson snapped, squaring his shoulders. 'I'm the law around here, not Charley Noonan.' As if to prove it he thrust out his left hand. 'I'll take that gun.'

Ebson lacked a few inches in height and could have used a bit more meat on his bones. His face was round and boyish, with eyes that kept flitting from one part of Rourke to another, as if afraid of missing something.

'No,' Rourke said quietly, 'I guess not.'

The outstretched hand dropped, the other shifting to the gun hanging low against the deputy's thigh. 'How was that?'

'Careful.' The warning came soft and cold.

Suddenly Ebson felt as if he was confronting an entirely different person. The man before him stood high, was hard-packed and flat-trimmed. His face, permanently scorched by many suns held no expression, but something there disturbed the deputy's self-assurance. His hand fell clear of the gun.

Rourke nodded, and stepped up on to the sidewalk.

'Thank you.' The voice came softly from the doorway of the general store, bringing him to a halt.

He swept off his hat. 'Ma'am. . . ?'

'For helping Billy,' she said.

Her hair was the colour of honey, shorter than most woman were wearing theirs, and, though proportioned with grace and care, she barely reached his shoulders. Rourke looked into blue eyes containing a soft shadow of sadness that momentarily robbed him of words. 'He . . . belong to you?'

'No,' she said, gathering her purse closer to her body, 'but I thank you nevertheless.' A flush was blossoming lightly on her cheeks as she turned quickly to re-enter the store.

With mounting anger, Ebson saw the girl move out of sight, Rourke fitting his hat back on his head as he continued without haste past Eli Fleischer's store, walking tall and erect, with the slight tilt of someone more accustomed to the saddle. He wanted to shout to stop him, to exert his authority, but he could manage none of those things. Memory of stone-grey eyes boring into him sent a wintry breeze sailing through the canyons of his mind.

A furtive movement jerked his gaze to the end of the alley, but whoever or whatever had been there was gone. Then a quiet snicker had him wheeling around. A couple of townsmen smiled broadly at him. Ebson felt a tightening in his chest, a crazy desire to lash out, to use the barrel of his pistol on both of them. Instead, acting as if they weren't there, he set out along the route Rourke had taken. With each step the back of his neck grew warmer; he knew that within hours a report of the past few minutes' events would be all over town.

It was the start of a new week and the saloons were not doing the sort of business they might have preferred. The Phoenix, the largest of the three, had a reasonable crowd, including Rourke who sat alone at a corner table, nursing a beer, listening to bits of conversation bouncing about the barnlike room. At the hotel he'd cleaned up, eaten in the dining-room, and then, as on the previous night drifted from one saloon to another.

For the past few minutes he'd been covertly watching a tall, fat man engaged in quiet conversation with the bartender, aware that, by way of the backbar mirror, he too was under scrutiny. The man was Frank Burrell, county sheriff. He'd found that out right after arriving in Redemption.

Draining the last of his beer, he started to scrape back his chair, quitting when he saw Burrell coming towards him.

Smiling, the fat man pulled one of the unused chairs away from the table. 'Mind if I join you, Mr Rourke?'

Rourke shrugged, watching the sheriff lower his bulk. It could, he thought, be dangerous to write this man off as either soft or flabby. The flesh on his moon-shaped face was smooth and tight and barely lined. The dark broadcloth suit and the black string tie lent him the appearance of a successful banker rather than a lawman. What spoiled the illusion was the wide cartridge belt circling his ample middle, pistol holstered butt-first for a cross-draw. He pushed his hat back to reveal thinning white hair.

'Got your name from the hotel register,' he said, resting plump hands upon the table. 'You have me curious, Mr Rourke. About what brings you here, I mean.'

'I could tell you I'm just passing through?'

Burrell ditched the smile. 'I'd sooner you didn't, 'cause I'd have a hard time believing it. No . . . you carry the smell of trouble, my friend.'

Rourke made no comment.

'I'm given to understand you've already had a run-in with my deputy.' Without providing any opportunity for a reply, Burrell said, 'But then, Manny's still young and a mite too cocksure of himself.'

Again Rourke offered nothing.

Dropping his hands from the table to his lap, Burrell leaned back. In an instant his already small eyes became hard black buttons and the genial banker image was gone. 'We're not too fond of strangers in Redemption. Not unless they have legitimate business. We're especially not fond of those toting guns and offering proof of their readiness to use them. You've been here two days, Rourke. You got in late Saturday, been eating breakfast at Kate's Kitchen instead of the hotel, after which you've fetched your horse from the stable and disappeared until almost dusk. So I'll ask again. What's your business here?'

Rourke picked up his empty glass, tilting it as though to be sure it was empty. With a slow sigh he lowered it back to the table. 'Looking over the country. Looking for a man.'

Burrell's mouth pulled down at the ends, thinning his lips. 'A goddamned bounty hunter.'

Rourke shook his head.

'Then what? If you're a lawman you should've checked with me when hitting town.'

Rourke shoved the glass to one side. 'Never claimed to be. Said I was looking for a man, that's all.'

'And when you find him?'

Rourke's shoulders gave a small, easy lift. 'That will be his decision. Either he comes back with me to stand trial, or . . .' He let the rest float.

'Or what?' Burrell snapped. 'You kill him?'

'That'll also be up to him.'

THREE

For a long while Burrell studied Rourke, never once blinking. 'You've got brass,' he said tightly. 'Forget who you're talking to?'

'Not for a moment.'

Impatiently, Burrell let out his breath. 'What's he supposed to've done, the one you're after?'

'Killed a girl. Accused her of trying to rob him when he was sleeping. Beat her up; left her for dead, then ran, leaving his money scattered over the floor of her room.'

'Where was this?'

'Place called Opulence.'

'Up north?'

'Uh-huh. Day's ride from Golconda,' Rourke nodded. 'Way it appears, after sneaking his horse and gear out of the livery stable, he kept running. Didn't stop until hitting Astoria before the town was yet awake. Broke into a store and shot the owner.'

'And got away with what?'

'Not a dime. The owner lived in rooms at back. Probably heard something, went to check, and got himself killed. One who did it must've again panicked and run.'

'Seems to me,' Burrell frowned sceptically, 'what I'm hearing is a whole lot of guesswork.'

'No, a bit more than that. I backtracked for weeks. Everything fits together. After killing the girl he cleared out in a hurry, leaving behind whatever money he had. Gives him a reason for busting into that store. He was broke and badly needing to get a long way from where he was.'

'And all this's supposed to've happened when?'

'Little over three months ago.'

The ridges in the big man's brow deepened. 'Been dragging your heels, haven't you?'

Rourke's response was another lift of his shoulders. 'Been somewhat tied up.'

'Next question.' Burrell leaned forward, resting thick arms on the table. 'What sort of reward's been put up?'

'None, far's I know.'

'Then what's the family offering you?'

'Isn't any. There was just him.'

'Then how come you're involved?'

'Because,' Rourke answered quietly, 'I promised someone I'd see whoever pulled that trigger fitted with a hang-rope.'

'Got a name – this someone?'

'Hatton. Wally Hatton.'

'Never heard of him,' Burrell said after giving the name some thought.

'No reason you should have.'

Once more the sheriff resorted to silence, allowing everything he'd heard to sink in. Finally he leaned back, head canted at the man across from him, as if to make sure he'd got his measure the first time. 'There more?'

'Couple more shootings I can tie him to. But they

can hold for a while.'

'And now you're getting round to telling me that this's where he was headed?'

Rourke answered with a slow nod.

'I'll want to hear the rest,' Burrell said, 'First, though—' Dipping into an inside coat pocket he produced a thin cigar, letting Rourke wait until he had it burning to his satisfaction. 'What's his name, the one you're after?'

'Tobin. Ken Tobin.'

'The girl give it to you?'

'Not to me; to those who found her.'

Burrell resurrected the frown. 'Got news for you, boy. Nobody in these parts using that handle. And I ought to know.'

'You going to try and stop me from taking him?' Rourke asked quietly, starting to roll a smoke of his own.

Examining the tip of his cigar, the sheriff smiled thinly. 'Didn't I just tell you nobody around here's got a name like that?'

This time it was Rourke who was silent. Then, watching for a reaction from the other side of the table, he asked, 'Diamond B, they a big outfit?'

Burrell wrenched the cigar from between his lips, spilling ash down the front of his coat. 'The biggest. The Ballentines are important people around here. I don't want you—'

Rourke never let him finish. 'That's who Tobin claimed to be riding for,' he said.

If not the best-designed, the main house at the Diamond B was surely the largest and most envied of all in the county. Starting as a one-room cabin, over the years it had been extended and improved until it stood two storeys high; a rambling collection of rooms under Spanish tiles, lavishly furnished by a woman who'd not had to worry about expense.

In the largest of those rooms, folded into one of the huge leather-covered chairs, Frank Burrell took the drink handed to him by Alecia Ballentine, smiling his thanks. 'My congratulations, Alecia,' he said respectfully. 'Understand you and Spense Harding have set a date.'

Alecia replied with a small smile and a quick nod, and Burrell could swear he saw a faint rush of colour to her cheeks.

A tall girl in the final years of her twenties, she was a shade less than slender. One of many respects in which she took after her mother. Her dark-green eyes were also those of Una Ballentine. Still, thought Burrell, a handsome enough woman, even if a little on the stern and skinny side to suit his tastes.

'Let's get back to this Rourke,' Jeff Ballentine grunted, seemingly irritated by mention of the forthcoming marriage.

Burrell lifted his eyes to the man who leaned against the wide stone fireplace, then above him to the painting of his late father and mother. He'd never considered it a good painting, but old Jake had been proud of it – even though he looked as phony as a store dummy in that fancy city suit, his wife as if she were at a funeral.

'Still don't understand,' Ballentine scowled. 'What made you think this important enough to ride out here tonight?'

'Thought it something you'd want to know.' Burrell tasted his drink, then took a larger swallow. 'There's a good chance he'll be out this way pretty soon. Thought I'd prepare you.'

'For what?' The scowl deepened, drawing thick brows tightly together. 'It doesn't concern me. If he wants to waste his time, let him.'

Not only was he the image of his father, thought Burrell, he even sounded like the old buffalo. A couple of years older than his sister, Jeff Ballentine was heavily built and starting to show a paunch. His face, a dark slab of flesh, bottomed out into a jutting chin. Dark hair was doing a fast retreat from his forehead, and under those heavy brows, smouldering eyes warned of an easily triggered anger.

'Not suggesting you have. Just thought I'd keep you posted . . . on account of him connecting this Tobin feller to the Diamond.'

'Because of what some floozy says? What some drunken hostler thinks he remembers?' Ballentine's snort was loaded with contempt. 'Some saddlebum claiming he works for us doesn't make it the truth. We've never had a Tobin on our payroll.'

'Which's what I told him. Said I'd have known if you had.' Burrell put on a puzzled expression. 'Didn't seem to faze him one little bit.'

Ballentine swallowed the rest of his drink in one impatient gulp, moving immediately to where an array of bottles stood on a handsome darkwood sideboard. 'Howie was up in Golconda for a couple of days round about then. We'd—'

'Never knew that,' Burrell said softly, his frown deepening.

'Well now you do,' Ballentine snapped irritably. 'We'd got word that rails were headed there, that it was to become a shipping point. Was my intention to send Maurie Kortman to check it out but— Well, Howie insisted he go. So I let him,' he said, voice dropping when his eyes flicked briefly to where his sister sat. *And because, like always when he wants something, he gets around her, gets her to pressure me.*

'He'd been working hard,' Alecia put in stiffly. 'He deserved a little time off.'

Ballentine splashed whiskey into his glass, more than he'd intended, then came back to stand before the sheriff. 'Anyway, we decided to keep it quiet until after we made our first drive. Never even told Kortman. Far's anyone knew Howie'd gone to visit with a distant relative.'

Watching them, listening to them, Burrell was once more reminded of who the real power at the Diamond was. Reluctantly he finished his drink and heaved himself upright.

'Maybe,' he said, addressing his words more to Alecia than her brother, 'the real reason I came out tonight is because there's something about this man I can't pin down. Says he's working strictly on his own, and probably he is. After he had a run-in with Manny—'

'One of these days,' Ballentine grunted derisively, 'that fool deputy is going to get his head blown off, the way he struts.'

'Might be,' Burrell agreed. 'Anyway, after I heard what happened, and while Rourke was out of the hotel, I helped myself to a look through his room. Nothing I found told me any more than I already know. Not that he'd be likely to leave anything like a badge lying around.' His eyes found a spot of interest at his feet. 'Still, can't rid myself of the feeling he's trouble waiting to happen.

'You're getting old, Frank – starting to let little things worry you.' Ballentine gave a small, mocking laugh. 'Or maybe it's the upcoming election. That it?

Worried those damn nesters will make trouble before then?'

'It's something I've considered,' Burrell confessed, his mind suddenly elsewhere. He put his gaze back on Ballentine. 'And it's something else we need to talk about, Jeff.'

'Some other time.' Ballentine attacked his fresh drink. 'Let's stick to this Rourke.' He wiped the back of his hand roughly across his mouth. 'If he worries you that much, get rid of him. Send him packing.'

'Might not be that easy,' Burrell sighed, depositing his glass on the fireplace mantel. 'Well – that's it. Thought it was something you'd want to know.'

Alecia stood up, smoothing her dress over honed-down hips. 'And I'm sure Jeff appreciates it.'

'Appreciates what?' a new voice queried, diverting attention to a pale-headed boy standing in the doorway.

'Where you been?' Ballentine snapped. 'You weren't at dinner again!'

'Out.' The boy smiled, coming into the room, stopping close to Alecia.

The youngest of the litter, Howard Ballentine, was nothing like either his brother or sister. Where they were dark, he was fair. Where they were tall, he was shorter and lighter, small-boned, with a round face and stubby nose. 'I miss something?' he asked, showing a line of fine white teeth.

'No,' Jeff answered, clearly nettled by the younger brother's offhanded attitude.

'Sheriff Burrell,' Alecia informed him, 'was telling us about a man in town looking for someone who claims to have been working for us.'

'Yeah?' Howie's tone became suddenly serious. 'Who?'

'Name we got is Tobin,' his brother supplied grudgingly. 'Claims he's wanted for a couple of killings.'

'He crazy!' Disbelief pitched Howie's voice high. 'There's nobody here with that name. Never has been.'

'What I've been telling him,' Ballentine said.

While looking at the youngest of the Ballentines, Burrell couldn't help but wonder if the difference in appearance may have had something to do with the age of his parents at the time of his conception. Howie had come along ten years after Jeff, and it was right after his birth that Una Ballentine's health started downhill.

'This Rourke feller,' he put in quietly, 'seems to think otherwise.'

FOUR

From the wide, railed veranda, the Ballentine brothers watched Burrell haul his bulk up into the saddle, doing so with the ease of a man half his weight. Once the sheriff was out of the yard, Howie made to move off.

Jeff clamped a hand on his shoulder and held him. 'This Tobin – you know him?'

Howie winced, tried to pull free, and couldn't. 'You crazy? What sort of dumb question is that?'

'Don't lie to me, little brother. I was watching you when his name came up. I saw your face.'

'You're nuts! I never—' The rest ended in a squeal when Jeff's fingers tightened. 'All right! *All right!* Up in Golconda – I think I ran into someone of that name.'

'Then why didn't you say so?'

'Because I wasn't sure. It was in a saloon – place called the Golden Arrow, I think. Had a bit too much to drink . . . heard someone talking, and there he was, next to me, being very sociable. Seem to recall him saying his name was Tobin.'

'Keep going,' Jeff said harshly.

'That's it damnit! I wasn't so drunk I couldn't peg

a panhandler. I bought him a couple, then shoved off. And that's the only time I ever saw him.'

'It better be. I find out different I'll nail your hide to the wall, just like I said I'd do if you cut up while away.'

'Why'd you think I didn't stick around?' Howie asked sullenly. 'Damnit, I told you – the place was busting at the seams. I couldn't even get a decent room.'

Jeff released him. 'He know who you were? – where you were from?'

Rubbing his shoulder, Howie squeezed up his face in thought. 'Don't know. If I somehow remember his name, I guess I might've told him mine.'

'If that's all there was to it, why didn't you tell Burrell?'

'What for? How'd it help? And why'd you tell him I was up there, anyway? Thought you said no one was yet to know?'

'I had my reasons,' Jeff growled, refusing to admit he'd made a mistake, that he'd spoken without thinking. 'You meeting up with this Tobin might explain how Diamond B's name got mixed up in that mess.' His focus swung back hard on Howie. 'There anything else you've forgotten to tell me?'

Still massaging his shoulder, Howie gave his brother a pained look. 'No, damnit! Why'd I lie about something like that? Why'd you think I decided to come back earlier than planned? Hell, you've still got to see Golconda. They got people there who'll steal your boots while you're walking in them! First night I was there my bag and the spare clothes I took along went missing!'

Jeff frowned down at his younger brother. 'Thought you told me the place was OK? Changing your mind?'

' 'Course not! They got holding corrals built, loading pens and ramps – everything. It'll save us time
and money making the next drive there. It's still a
little wild, but no worse than Abilene. Like I told you,
the place was overcrowded, everyone trying to turn a
fast profit. Getting a meal or a drink was as tough as
finding a place to bunk! Which's about when I
decided to start back home while I still had some
money left.'

'And Opulence? What'd you think of it?'

Howie let him see the question made no sense.
'What's that?'

'A town, a half-day's ride east of Golconda.'

Howie shook his head. 'Wasn't on the stage route.'

Jeff had another question, but seeing Maurie
Kortman coming from the barn, he skipped it and
called to the foreman. Kortman glanced up, then
started for the house.

Quietly, Howie went back inside.

Halting in front of the veranda, Kortman tilted his
narrow face up at his employer. 'Want me?' Tall and
lean as a telegraph pole, he'd started at the Diamond
when old Jake was still the boss.

'Saw Noonan ride out with Mayo and Amherst
right after supper,' Jeff told him, allowing the state-
ment to pose his question.

'Said they had business in town.' Kortman
shrugged, squinty eyes narrowing, anticipating
Ballentine's next question. 'Figured it kind of odd,
but it was their affair, their time.'

Coming out of the Phoenix, Rourke lingered at the
edge of the sidewalk to finish his smoke. There were
few horses at the tie rack, even fewer elsewhere along
the street. Light fanned out from windows of stores

still open for business, the brightest coming from
Fleischer's. In front of the emporium a stout woman
was using both hands and mouth to dispense directions to a man and boy loading their purchases on to
a tired-looking wagon. Back in the saloon sporadic
laughter erupted, while somewhere further away a
dog's yapping accompanied a piano that sounded as
if it had keys missing. From the very tail-end of the
town came the intermittent clanging of the blacksmith's late-working hammer.

Another night in another town, a time when,
surrounded by buildings and people, the full weight
of loneliness would settle down upon him. The night
was still young but he had nowhere to go, no one to
go to.

Batwings swished open and shut when someone
else emerged from the saloon. A heavy-shouldered,
long-armed man stood momentarily undecided,
then angled off away from Rourke.

As so often she did, with neither invitation nor
welcome, Loretta invaded his thoughts. Beautiful
Loretta, the apple of her parents' eyes. Lying, deceiv-
ing Loretta Videll. He wondered where she was this
night, what she might be doing. . . .

It puzzled him that such thoughts would still
spring from ambush, for no longer did he feel
anything for her. Even the anger and disgust had
long ago flickered and died. So why did he still think
about her? It had been years, almost half his lifetime,
since she had shared his name. And then for only so
short a time.

Spinning the cigarette butt into the street he
jerked down the curtain on the memory.

More puzzling was the fact that thoughts of
Loretta would surface so easily when the thing he

tried hard to remember about Wally Hatton continued to be stubbornly elusive. It was important, of that
he was certain, but whatever it was, it remained
deeply buried in some cavern of his mind.

The man and boy were through loading, closing
the tailgate. He watched while they helped the
woman up on to the wagon-seat, and for some reason
it brought his thoughts to a skinny old man, frightened, and a little strange. And a girl with hair the
colour of fresh honey, whose depthless blue eyes
held a hint of sadness and concern. He straightened,
flicked another glance along the opposite side of the
street, and without thinking too much about it,
turned himself in the direction of Fleischer's store.

Behind the counter a man of late middle age was
making entries into a small book, getting ready, it
seemed, to close shop. Rourke's gaze shuttled slowly
around the store but found no one else present. He
bought tobacco and matches, and left. It had been
stupid to think the girl might work there.

Back on the sidewalk he took time to carefully
build another cigarette before continuing on past
the store, his pace leisurely maintained until arriving
at the end of the next block. From there on the only
lights were a pair of lanterns, one on each side of the
entrance to Kramer's Stable & Feed Barn, and,
beyond, a square glow from the blacksmith's doorway. The moon remained a dull silver ball behind the
low cloud-bank.

He stopped, studying the gloom on the other side
of the street, got rid of the half-smoked cigarette and
heeled slowly about.

'This do?'

Across the wide street a shadow appeared to
quickly shift. A few yards in front of him another

pulled free from a recessed doorway. Faint light at its rear created a silhouette of someone with broad shoulders and long arms dangling close to his sides. 'Just fine,' a deep voice rumbled. 'Just fine!' With the last words still leaving his mouth the dark form began a headlong charge, boots striking hard against the wooden boards.

Bracing himself for the attack, Rourke was suddenly jolted forward by someone unseen and unheard ramming heavily into his back, almost knocking him off his feet.

Unbalanced, he stumbled straight into the fist of the one coming at him. The blow skimmed off the side of his face, jarring him backward – into another pair of hands that grabbed and dragged him off the sidewalk and into the dust of the alley. He hit the ground hard, rolled, tried to get back on to his feet and a voice snapped, 'Keep the bastard down! Dave, get his gun!'

A boot drove itself into his side, spinning him over on to his face, pain wrenching a groan from his throat. One of them emptied his holster and tossed the gun deep into the darkness of the alley. He made another try to get up, and they let him, waiting until he was on his knees before closing in. The one so handy with his boots led the pack. Poor light continued to conceal his features when he stopped, brought back a leg, and let fly with another kick.

But this time his victim was better prepared. When it was only inches from his chest Rourke caught the boot in both hands, gave it a violent twist and, holding on, used the man's failing weight to help lever himself upward. The one with the long arms stepped quickly aside to avoid colliding with his downed companion. Then he came at Rourke, right fist swinging wide and wild.

Rourke ducked, lowered his head, and hit him in the middle like a battering ram. He rolled backward, grunting and gasping, and Rourke closed in, bringing up a fist from down low, smashing it squarely into the other's face. He felt something crunch and collapse under his knuckles, heard a howl of pain, and moved quickly back.

The one who'd hauled him off the walk was vertical again, making a groggy attempt to attack from behind. Rourke pivoted, drove an elbow backward and brought his attacker to a staggering stop and a groaning retreat.

He'd made a mistake believing there'd been only two – one following from the rear, the other from across the street. Somewhere ahead there'd been a third, the one holding a hand to his mouth, spluttering and spitting. His eyes raked the dark, but it was his ears that located the third party when a furious curse exploded at his back. He whipped around, but before the turn was half-way done a thing harder than any human fist cracked against his head, knocking him sideways.

A blaze of white flared up inside his skull and unhinged his legs. The gun barrel lifted again and for one brief second he had a flash of a round, hate-filled face. The gun came at him again, but this time he barely felt the blow.

Somewhere in the thick, swirling darkness that wrapped itself around him, he heard a shot.

Like echoes from a long, narrow tunnel came the sound of footsteps, disjointed voices ... Then his eyes were suddenly open, his mind scraping together fragments of memory. The moon appeared to have found a small break in the clouds, for the alley was no longer as dark as it had been. He lay still, listening, eyes fastened on a thing that was somehow familiar and yet, no matter how hard he stared, trying to make sense of it, remained a shapeless bundle pressed up against the opposite wall.

The footsteps were ringing louder against the walk, almost at the alley's mouth. He dragged his hands through the dirt, and pushed up, the effort threatening to burst his skull. A short distance away he sensed movement – through a greasy haze saw the shapeless thing stretch upward and sprout arms and legs. Something in one of its hands gave off a dull glint.

He managed to raise himself to his knees, and when two figures appeared at the mouth of the alley, he was finally upright, trying to keep the ground from shifting under his feet. A man and a woman drew closer. They stopped, the woman speaking softly before moving away. Then the man was in front of him, big and broad.

'Think you can walk?'

Rourke nodded, instantly regretting the move. 'I'm OK.'

'Sure you are,' the man grunted. 'But let's make certain.'

He went on speaking, but Rourke was more interested in the woman who'd stepped into the darker shadows. He could hear her voice, but her words were just distant sounds.

A hand fell on his shoulder, gave him a slight shake. 'I asked if you could walk back to my office.'

His name was Jim Sturret, a large, heavily built block

of a man with a broad, clean-shaven face and iron-grey hair. All the while he'd been working he'd been grunting comments to which Rourke, his mind elsewhere, had paid little attention.

'Don't listen too well, do you?' Sturret asked gruffly, dumping the stuff he'd been working with on to a glass-topped table at his left. 'I said your head must be made of rock. You've got a couple of bumps which are going to give you merry hell for a while, but you'll survive. Won't even need a bandage.'

Rourke started to rise. 'Thanks, Doc. Appreciate the help.'

Sturret pushed him back down. 'Rest – and don't thank me. It's Miss Terry who fetched me.' Seeing Rourke's forehead give birth to a frown, he said, 'Ellen Terry. Runs a boarding-house on Coronado Street, not far from where you were—' He broke off, picked up a towel and needlessly wiped his hands. 'Exactly what did happen to you?'

'Ran into a man,' Rourke answered quietly.

'Who apparently didn't care much for the shape of your skull,' Sturret grunted irritably, realizing he'd get no more. He threw aside the towel and adjusted his half-lens spectacles. 'Think you could risk giving me your name?'

Rourke gave it to him. 'How'd she find me?'

'Wasn't her that did. Old Billy Deacon – he saw what was going on and went to call her – her being one of very few people he trusts.'

'The old-timer – the mute?'

Sturret was about to turn away when he stopped. 'He's not dumb. Leastways he wasn't born that way. Way I got it wagon-train his folks were on was attacked by Apaches. Billy, like everyone else, was left for dead, his throat slashed. How he survived is a miracle, though he's never been able to speak properly since.' Sturret finished the turn, moved to a roll-top desk, and when coming around again held a gun in one hand, a black hat in the other. 'He found these – figured they belong to you.'

Rourke put aside the hat, took the Colt, held it a moment, then thumbed back the gate and checked the loads in the cylinder. Two chambers held spent shells.

Now it was Sturret who was frowning. 'Something wrong?'

Rourke risked another head-shake. Reaching for fresh loads from his belt, he discovered the front of his shirt was wide open. He put down the gun.

'Checked you over for other injuries, remember?' Sturret reminded him. 'Few bad bruises, but they'll go away.' He removed his glasses, using thick fingers to tightly pinch the bridge of his nose. 'Stopped a couple of slugs in your time, haven't you? Know those sort of scars.' He hesitated before going on. 'But the one across your chest . . . that's something else.'

Pretending he'd heard neither the remark nor the question it conveyed, Rourke buttoned his shirt, repacked the gun's chambers, and stood up. His head throbbed and his ribs hurt, but he could focus and think more clearly now.

Sturret stood by, watching closely, not saying a word until he reached for his hat. 'What happened – it doesn't seem to be bothering you much.'

Rourke adjusted the holster against his leg. 'It's something that can be taken care of,' he said.

FIVE

It boasted no sign, but it was the most imposing house along Coronado, and big enough to look as if it might be a boarding-house. Even in the thickly filtered moonlight the paint on both building and picket-fence bore a fresh look. The shrubbery was neat and skillfully trimmed – everything cloaked in an atmosphere of subtle respectability. Light glowed softly behind a frosted-glass panel in the door. Rourke yanked the bell-pull, and waited. The cool night air had cleared his head, but the aching throb persisted.

At the sound of soft, approaching footsteps, he removed his hat. Until then he'd not considered the possibility of anyone but her opening the door, yet when she did he experienced pleasant surprise.

'Miss Terry?'

'Yes. . . ?'

'Stopped by to say thanks,' he said, and told her his name.

Her head tilted in momentary confusion. Then, with sudden understanding, she said, 'Oh, I'm sorry. I was busy in the kitchen. I'm afraid part of my mind is still there.' She studied his face, saw the darkening bruise along his cheekbone. 'You're – all right?'

'Fine,' he lied, hands tightly rolling the brim of his hat. 'Well . . . just wanted to say thanks. Appreciate what you did. You and the old-timer.'

'It was nothing,' she said quickly. 'Anyone would have done the same.' She stepped back, opening the door wider. 'I – I've made fresh coffee. If you don't mind sitting in the kitchen, you're very welcome to a cup.'

A while later, dawdling over a second cup, he watched her finishing the last of her chores, admiring the efficiency and grace of her movements, unable to remember ever having enjoyed the company of anyone like Ellen Terry. Petite of build, yet exhibiting both a physical and spiritual strength, she was, Rourke imagined, somewhere in her mid-twenties. And more than just attractive.

She turned from the sink, took off her apron and joined him at the table. 'Billy doesn't live here,' she said by way of answering his question. 'In fact, I don't think anyone really knows where he lives. What Dr Sturrett told you about him is as much as I know. That, and the fact that his inability to communicate normally makes it difficult for him to find work. Especially,' she added with some bitterness, 'since the likes of that awful Charley Noonan, started saying he's a thief and not to be trusted.'

While she talked Rourke was trying to fathom the gravity, the touch of sadness that lay deep in her eyes. 'An opinion. I gather, you don't share.'

'One I totally reject! Billy has yet to be caught stealing anything.' She lifted her shoulders, wearily letting them fall. 'But few seem to really care about the truth, or whether he lives or dies.'

'You care,' he said quietly.

'And so do a few others. We feed him when he comes around – do what little we can. But,' – and now the tiredness reflected on her face was starting to make itself heard in her voice – 'Billy maintains his distance, refuses to let himself get too close to anyone.'

Reluctantly, Rourke slid back his chair and stood up. Pain rolled through his head, punched at the inner walls of his skull. Until then he'd forgotten all about it. Talking with her had been so easy, like something done times before. In her he'd found no evidence of pretence, only poise and simplicity. 'Seems he trusts you, Miss Terry.'

'I'd like to think so,' she said, also rising. 'He often does odd jobs for me. And usually very well.'

'Gather he can also . . . well, talk to you.'

She answered with a small smile. 'Billy Deacon may have an affliction, Mr Rourke, but he's far from stupid. He can make himself understood when he wishes to. And he understands a great deal more than he's credited for.'

'Like he proved tonight?'

Ellen Terry nodded. 'I've no idea what he was doing in that alley – but he was there, and he saw what was happening and came running to me. You see, he remembered you from this afternoon's incident.' She paused, the tiniest of frowns tracing itself on to her brow. 'Is that why you were attacked? Because of what happened then?'

'Not sure,' Rourke smiled bleakly. 'They never told me.'

He picked up his hat from where he'd placed it on the floor. All the time he'd been there he'd been curious as to how a girl of her years and obvious education came to be operating a boarding-house,

but he'd backed away from asking. Now, about to ask
if the old man had told her of finding his gun and
firing it at the three who'd attacked him, he again
backed off.

At the front door he thanked her once more, this
time offering his hand. The smallness and coolness
of hers made him afraid to hold it too long for fear
of crushing it.

Maurie Kortman was the last to come in for breakfast. He'd had a bad night and was not in the best of
moods. A feeling of impending trouble was riding
him, annoying him because he could find no explanation for it. He took his place at the head of the
long, scrubbed pine table, grunting a curt 'Mornin'
without looking at any of the crew. Only when the
cocinero dumped a loaded plate in front of him did he
become conscious of the uncharacteristic silence. He
raised his head, slowly shifting his gaze from man to
man, passing lightly over those on his left, older
hands, men who'd been at the Diamond almost as
long as he, pausing when reaching the two at the far
end of the table.

Resentment again brought a rigidity to Kortman's
jaw. Jesse Vance and Burt Dwyer could have been cast
from the same mould. Thin, hawk-faced men who
spoke little to anyone but each other, and answered
only to Ballentine. They'd arrived at the Diamond
late Sunday and in that time he'd shared no more
than a dozen words with them. He knew why they
were there, and had little liking for the reason. But
right then it was the trio seated on his right who held
his interest.

Nearest was Les Mayo, whose greeny-brown eyes

always made him think of moss on pebbles. Not yet thirty, Mayo was already losing his hair, looking middle-aged. He kept his head down, but Kortman hadn't missed the split and swollen lower lip. His eyes flicked to Charley Noonan, the next man. On the surface a chubby, easy-going type, but one who, in the blink of an eye, could become as deadly as a stepped-on rattler. This morning Noonan appeared preoccupied with the food on his plate.

On Noonan's right sat Dave Amherst, broad shoulders hunched. Above a drooping moustache his nose was red and swollen to twice its normal size, the nostrils stuffed with bits of rag.

'All right,' the whip-lean ramrod drawled, 'I'm listening.'

'Ain't nothin',' Noonan answered dourly. 'Disagreement with a couple fellers, is all. Got a bit rough.'

Kortman kept his slit-eyed glare on Amherst. 'Broken?'

'And hurting like hell,' the other mumbled, gingerly fingering his nose.

'Never occurred to you to see the doc while you were still in town, did it?' Kortman asked, making an effort to keep from exploding. 'Now it'll mean another trip back – and on a day when I'll be needing all of you.'

'I can work,' Amherst returned sullenly. 'I don't need to see no croaker.'

'The hell you don't!' Kortman snapped. 'Go on, damnit! Eat your grub, then saddle up.'

Amherst was given no chance to argue for another voice was calling to Kortman moments before its owner showed himself at the galley door. 'Maurie? You in there?'

Kortman swung around moodily. 'Where else would I be this time of morning?'

'Jeff wants to see you when you're through,' Howie Ballentine announced, his small, round face darkening, wanting to remind the foreman of his place at the Diamond. But he said nothing, turning his attention instead to the others, grinning when his gaze fell upon Amherst. 'What the hell happened to you?'

'Boys had a little trouble in town,' Kortman told him in blunted tones.

'Yeah? With who?'

'Nobody you'd know, Howie.' Kortman reached for his knife and fork. 'Tell your brother I'll be along shortly.'

Another deep flush rose high in Howie's face. His mouth moved, but when the words still refused to come he spun around and left, fury rising swiftly to the boil. *One day, Kortman . . . One day . . . !* Behind him he heard a soft chuckle. *You, too, Noonan . . . you too!*

Tom Harding had many times visited Diamond B headquarters, but seldom without experiencing a pang of resentment at that which greeted him. He and Jake Ballentine had been the first to establish themselves here, long before any of the other cattlemen moved in, long before anyone had given a thought to county status. They'd been rough and lean, those early years, but not only had they made it, they'd become the most respected men in the community. It was Ballentine, though, proving himself a shrewd manipulator of men, money, and opportunity, who was the one to seize the power, using it to further advance his ambitions.

Each time Harding viewed the large house standing in the shade of several pepper-trees, remembering how it had begun, the feeling that something had been cleverly put over on him took deeper root. He sat his horse on the low hill west of the ranch, gazing down on to the sheds and barns, neatly and orderly arranged and in top-notch repair. Flowers showed a mild profusion of colour around the house, while beyond, rows of shaggy poplars stood like fifty-foot sentinels watching over a huge vegetable garden and a peach-orchard.

On their way to the Diamond they'd had to pass the old JT spread and its abandoned buildings. Three years ago, soon after Jack Terry was killed, Ballentine had acquired it, buying it so he'd have the only unhindered access to Jacinto Flats.

A stocky, grizzled man with a ruddy-complexioned bulldog face, Tom Harding, brought his attention back to the house, remembering the woman Jake Ballentine had taken for his wife. She'd been Una Nicholas when Harding first met her, a woman of strong will and purpose. He straightened suddenly, pinched out his cigarette, and turned to the silent young man beside him.

'Might's well go on down,' he grunted, feeling another of those cursed headaches coming on.

'Might's well.' But his son did not move.

'Waiting for something?' Harding frowned.

Spenser Harding, tall, well-packed and handsome in a bland sort of way, rubbed his chin and declined to look at his father. 'You know why Jeff asked you to ride over with me, don't you?'

Tom Harding gave a short, forced chuckle. 'When'd you start getting the idea I was stupid? 'Course I do – he wants to be sure he can count on us to side him in getting those damn nesters off the flats.'

'Will you?'

The older man was a while in answering. 'Don't see as I've much choice, what with Alecia about to become my daughter-in-law. Be like supporting family – though Diamond's the only outfit that'll benefit. They're the one's using it as part of their range.'

Spense nodded in agreement. 'But we let them drift in the way they're starting to, they'll quickly become our problem, too. Every cattleman's problem.'

'Can hear who's been bending your ear,' Harding grunted, the ache in his head mounting. 'What Jeff kind of forgets, though, is the valley's government land, always has been. Those sodbusters are within their rights. I talked to Burrell about it.'

Leather creaked when the younger Harding shifted uncomfortably. 'Burrell will do what Jeff tells him.'

'Uh-huh, because right now he knows which side his bread's buttered. But he's sweating, Spense – in case those grangers put up a squawk and a US Marshal's sent down here.'

Howie Ballentine came out of the house to linger on the veranda for a minute or two. He'd had enough of listening to the palaver, enough of having his suggestions and comments brushed aside by Jeff and that red-faced old bugger. Even Maurie Kortman, no more than a hired hand, acted as if he wasn't there. Only Alecia and Spense had made any attempt to listen to what he'd had to offer, and Spense had probably done so just to keep in good with Alecia.

He went down the steps, into the yard, trying to understand what it was his sister saw in the fellow. Spense was big and okay to look at, but there was a softness in him. A gentleness Alecia called it. Well, he knew different. Spense Harding was a tad short on guts, which is why he never questioned any order his father dished out. But he was Alecia's choice, her problem.

Reaching the centre of the broad yard, he stopped, wondering what chance he had of slipping away without his absence being noticed.

The place seemed unusually quiet that time of morning. Even the breeze sighing through the trees, the occasional metallic creak of the windmills was louder than the muted sounds coming from the cookshack and blacksmith shop. He started to move again, halting after only a single step.

From somewhere behind him came the soft, barely discernible clink of a bridle chain. Howie heeled sharply about, coming to a stop with a sudden intake of breath.

On the far side of the yard, in the shade of a giant cottonwood, stood a horse, big and almost black in the screened light. The man sitting loosely in saddle while rolling up a smoke was tall, solidly built, and what showed of his face under the black hat, deeply bronzed. Howie had not heard him arrive, had no idea how long he'd been there.

Slowly he let out his breath. The man's attire marked him as just another puncher, probably riding the grub line. But when the blue roan was stepped forward, further into the yard, instinct sent a warning rippling through the boy. This was no drifter, no saddlebum – not on that animal!

This was the one the sheriff had warned them of.

SIX

The rider pulled up a few feet from where the youngest of the Ballentines remained planted and unmoving.

'Boss man around?'

Howie swallowed, swallowed again and tried to get moisture back into his mouth. 'In the house,' he managed, cursing the rasp of his voice. 'Looking – for work?'

'No, just a little of his time.'

Howie took a few reverse steps. 'What name do I say?' he asked, though already certain what it would be.

Rourke gave it to him, not missing the slight stiffening of the boy's light frame.

For a long breath Howie could only stare at the man frowning down at him, positive he'd never seen him before, but at the same time recognizing an intangible something that put a further chill on the cold knot in his stomach. With an effort he straightened up, bracing narrow shoulders. 'I'll get him,' he said, already turning away.

Rourke finished his smoke, stepped the big roan closer to the house, and remained mounted.

Eventually a man with thick brows and jutting chin appeared in the doorway, then came on to the veranda and up to the railing. Behind him trailed the blond boy.

'Howie here says you want to see me.'

Rourke gave a small nod. 'If you own this spread.'

'I'm Jeff Ballentine, and I'm in the middle of a meeting. So what's it you want?'

'Looking for someone,' Rourke replied, realizing there'd be no invitation to step down. 'Information I've got is that he worked for your outfit.'

A tall, reed-like number had followed the boy from the house. Propping his back against the wall he fixed slit eyes hard upon Rourke, making note of all they saw. Now came a slender, dark-haired woman accompanied by a solidly constructed young man wearing an expression of mild perplexity. Together they moved to Ballentine's right, as though to lend him support.

'Lots of men have worked for us,' Ballentine said.

'This one uses the name Ken Tobin.'

A cautious interval of thought passed before Ballentine shook his head. 'No one of that handle here. Never has been.'

'Never said he was a man,' Rourke returned easily. 'Critter I want is a back-shooting horse thief – who'd clean out the pockets of dead men.'

'Easy there!' The one standing beside the thin woman spoke up sharply. 'There happens to be a lady present!'

Alecia Ballentine placed a hand on his arm. 'It's all right, Spense. I've heard worse from my father.'

Rourke reached up and tipped back his hat. 'My apologies. Had no intention of offending you.'

'You haven't.' She threw a quick, sideways glance

at Ballentine before asking, 'You're some kind of law officer?'

'No. It's personal. One of those Tobin killed was a friend.'

Ballentine took a grip on the railing, leaning himself forward. 'Exactly what made you think you'd find him here?'

The corners of Rourke's mouth creased in the hint of a smile. 'Had an idea the sheriff would have told you why.'

'Yeah, something about—' Ballentine's lips abruptly compressed.

'—a girl being beaten to death in a place called Opulence,' Rourke finished for him.

'All right but I still don't see what the blazes it has to do with me.'

'Figured he'd also have told you about a horse being sneaked out of the stable while the hostler was sleeping.'

'He mentioned it!' Ballentine snapped. 'Also mentioned the man had been drinking.'

'True,' Rourke nodded. 'Thing that interested me, though, was the fact that whoever took the horse must've had a pretty important reason for doing so. Like maybe not wanting its brand seen.'

Ballentine pulled himself up straight, waving a hand of dismissal. 'Would've made no difference to me if it had.'

'Probably not. But up in Golconda, the closest town to Opulence, I learned about this Tobin claiming to be one of your top hands. Tobin, as the sheriff surely told you, was the name the girl used to tag the one who beat her up.'

Ballentine swung around to confront the man leaning close to the door. 'Maurie – tell him!'

Kortman pushed up straight. 'You heard what the boss told you. Anyone says different is a liar. We've had no riders up that way, but we've sure as hell had our share of horseflesh stolen over the years!'

'Good enough,' Rourke shrugged. 'I'll accept that. Until something turns up to tell me different.'

Ballentine's face darkened, but the intervention of his sister prevented him saying anything.

'As I understand it,' she said, thin eyebrows arching, 'the woman who was killed was a – a saloon girl, or something of that nature. Was she the friend you mentioned?'

Rourke turned slowly to give her his complete attention and whatever it was Alecia Ballentine discovered in those grey eyes made her avert her own. Next to her, Spenser Harding looked even more confused by the things he was hearing.

'Not sure it matters what she was,' Rourke answered quietly. 'But, no, ma'am, I never knew her; know nothing about her. His name was Wally Hatton, the friend I'm talking about – a man getting on in years, looking forward to settling down.' A shadow moved behind the lace curtains at the window in front of which Alecia and Harding stood, telling Rourke that another party was watching and listening. He waited a moment before going on.

'Wally and his partner were camped in the hills a few miles from Astoria when someone bust into their camp and shot them both. Wally got it twice in the back. His partner in the chest. Afterwards, the one who'd bushwhacked them cleared off with their horses, most of their provisions . . . and a money-belt holding just over three thousand in bank-notes.'

Again there was a prolonged silence before Spenser Harding, eyes and brow a display of puzzlement, spoke up. 'The partner . . . That was you?'

Ballentine shoved a harsh glare at him, then turned back to Rourke who answered the question with a slow nod.

'Uh-huh. I was the one stripped of the money-belt.' He saw the narrowing of Ballentine's eyes, the pallid face of his younger brother, and lifted reins, starting to back the roan away from the house. 'Appreciate your time. Your . . . hospitality.'

In his wake he heard Ballentine's call, but when stopping to hitch himself around in the saddle, it was to ask, 'Fellow named Noonan works for you, right?'

Forgetting his own question, Ballentine asked, 'What of it?'

'Just wanted to be sure.' Rourke gave the gelding's flanks a gentle touch of steel. But not before noticing how mention of Noonan had pulled the one called Maurie closer to the veranda's edge.

They were still grouped there when Tom Harding emerged from the house, forehead deeply furrowed. 'What was that all about?'

Ballentine came slowly around, growling, 'I'll tell you inside.'

The old man stayed where he was, squinting at the diminishing image of Rourke. 'Not the last you'll be seeing of that feller, Jeff. Mark my words – that's trouble you got there.' He turned slowly to face his host. 'OK, let's go in. Got a headache that's driving me nuts!'

'You need glasses,' Ballentine grunted irritably, leading the way back into the house.

The younger Harding held back. Alecia, noticing this, stopped when reaching the front door, turned and found him and her younger brother quietly contemplating each other.

'You were up in Golconda a few months back, weren't you?' Harding asked cautiously.

'Back off Spense!' Howie snarled. 'Don't you start on me!'

From the doorway of the tack room Ballentine watched Spense leave the house and stride stiffly to his waiting horse, taking note of the fact that Alecia was not on hand to see him off. An hour earlier, presumably to give his son a little time with his future daughter-in-law, Tom Harding had started back home.

Minutes later, when entering the large front room, Ballentine found his sister seated on the couch, noisily flipping the pages of a magazine.

He poured himself a drink and carried it to the fireplace. She did not look up. 'Trouble in Loveland?' he asked.

Angrily, Alecia threw aside the magazine. 'Don't try to be clever, Jeff. It doesn't suit you.'

Her brother's long face darkened. He took a sip of the whiskey and held his peace.

'All right,' she snapped. 'We had a little tiff, but it's nothing he won't get over.' Calming down a little, she said, 'It's that man – that Rourke. He has me on edge, and poor Spense got the brunt of my mood.' She retrieved the magazine, gave it a brief scan, before again tossing it aside. 'Burrell was right about him. So was Spense's father. He's going to be troublesome.'

Jeff watched his sister rise, hands clasping together below a narrow waist and it suddenly occurred to him that he could not recall ever seeing her in anything but a dress. His gaze skipped briefly to the discarded magazine, then back to her. Just like the women pictured in those stupid things she read. 'Got a feeling you're right,' he said, slowly bobbing his head.

'I know I am!' Her mouth drew into an almost lipless line and for several uncomfortable seconds she was silent, eyes fixed on her brother, but seeing only images resurrected in memory. 'I've been thinking about what he told us – about being ambushed and robbed.'

Jeff took another pull at his drink, eyes narrowing under heavy brows. 'What about it?'

'Howie had money when he returned from that trip, remember? I've no idea how much, but it was fairly substantial.'

'Claimed he got lucky,' Jeff shrugged. 'Said he picked it up at a poker table.'

'I know what he *said*,' she retorted. 'I also remember what I overheard him telling you last night, after Burrell left.'

Jeff's face went blank.

'He said he decided to start back for home *while he still had some money left.*'

'Probably talking about what he won.'

'That's possible,' Alecia conceded. Once more she fell to brief silence, her stance unchanged. Finally she asked, 'Do you believe him?'

The glass stopped half-way to Ballentine's mouth. 'Hell, come on, Sis! If he says it happened that way . . .'

'Jeff,' she said patiently, 'We both know our younger brother, and we know of all the scrapes he's been in.'

'Damnit Alecia, he was still a kid then! He was wild, just starting to feel his oats!'

Alecia's chin lifted. 'He's still young, and not very much changed.'

Jeff gulped down what was left of his drink. 'You're crazy!' he growled loudly. 'There's no proof! And' – his voice dropped, became thoughtful – 'even if there was, it was you who talked me into letting him go up there. I was dead against it, but you—'

'I've not forgotten.' Alecia's hands came apart. She turned from him, moving to the window to gaze out into the yard. 'Nor that in a few weeks I'll be marrying Spense – or that you have problems of your own with those cursed farmers.'

The reminder of the recent influx of homesteaders, filing on what until recently had been regarded as free range, had Ballentine's big hand almost crushing the glass it held. The grass was important to Diamond's continued growth, and like most other cattlemen, he knew what would happen if those stinking sodbusters were permitted to go ahead and fence off and carve up the land. Somehow they had to be driven out, but so far the only plan he'd been able to come up with was being challenged by the law – the very law his father had installed, which Ballentine money and power still kept in office.

'What are you trying to tell me?' he asked.

Alecia's slim form slowly turned and the total lack of expression on her thin face, the coolness of her reply, startled him. It was like seeing and hearing his mother again.

She said, 'This Rourke is just one man, but he could succeed in stirring up enough trouble to ruin both our plans – even bring down the reputation and everything the Ballentine family has ever represented. He's just one man, Jeff. It shouldn't be all that difficult to – to take care of him.'

It was a while before Ballentine could speak. 'You mean—'

Alecia raised a hand to silence him. 'I don't need to know the details. I'm sure you can think of something. If you can't . . . perhaps Noonan, or those two new men you've hired could offer a suggestion.'

A hard man whose life had not been without violence, whose mind, even at that moment, was partly focused on another strike against the new settlers, Ballentine could but stare at his sister, having difficulty believing what he'd just heard. He started to speak, but stopped when remembering something he'd meant to ask Rourke, and hadn't. He raised the tightly held glass, realized it was empty, and said, 'There's something you maybe never noticed out there.'

Lips still drawn fight, Alecia's head went back. 'And what would that be?'

'If Howie'd been in any way involved with the things Rourke claims, how come Rourke never recognized him? Or, for that matter, how come Howie never remembered him?'

'I've no idea,' Alecia admitted. 'But I still believe that unless stopped, that man will be trouble. It's up to you to do so, Jeff, and to do it before it's too late.'

The pain-dulling effects of the drinks downed in the Phoenix were worn off, and though letting the horse carry him home at a leisurely walk, each time a hoof met the ground it sent pain jolting through Amherst's nose and across his eyes. Adding to his misery, the court plaster the sawbones had used was itching and pulling at his skin. He swore loudly, pulled rein, and fumbled in his pockets for papers and tobacco.

He'd stopped on the extreme curve of a switch-back from where he could see down into the basin, on to the trail ribboning out below. But he'd travelled that way many a time, and so, with his attention full upon the task of shaping up a smoke, he paid it no mind. Not until he had the quirly between his lips and was searching for a match did he see the rider.

The distance was still too great to recognize whoever rode the blue roan, but some inexplicable instinct had Amherst slow his movements.

With the cigarette lighted, he backed the horse out of sight, but not so far back that he could no longer see who was coming towards him. He waited, sucking hungrily on the cigarette, then, just as the rider below took the turn that would carry him from view, Amherst knew for sure whom he was watching.

This time when he swore it was quieter, but far more venomous. Hastily his eyes searched the terrain and found nothing of what he sought. Remembering a heavy outcropping of rock passed only minutes ago, he got the horse turned and stepping.

Snatching the Winchester from its boot, he cursed again, but this time with a perverted satisfaction, and wholly unconscious of pain. This was where he settled things in a way that would more than make up for a busted nose.

SEVEN

Rourke wasn't sure if he'd discovered anything other than that there'd been no welcome for him at the Ballentine ranch. He'd not learned who the woman and her companion were, except that whoever she was, she had the air of one who exercised a certain authority. The squinty-eyed stringbean looked and acted like one of the ranch crew, possibly the ramrod; the jumpy yellow-haired boy as if he'd been well-taught regarding his place in the order of things. He couldn't even guess who'd been behind the curtain.

Yet, in spite of the denials, he couldn't shake the feeling that there existed a meaningful connection between Tobin and the Diamond B. Ballentine had brushed the matter aside too easily. He'd not even asked for a description of the man. Which, Rourke reminded himself was just as well. The descriptions he'd picked up in Golconda were vague and contradictory, and worth little.

The town had been overflowing at the time, with everyone focused on their own affairs, their own objectives. It was still bustling when he got there, and few had been willing to waste time listening to questions. Most had backed off, regarding him with the suspicion and contempt reserved for badge-toters. The big slob hired as town marshal had been as helpful as a broken leg.

Only a barman at the smallest of the saloons had any recollection of value. And then only because some bum calling himself Tobin and claiming to be a rider for a big-shot outfit – Diamond-something-or-other – had tried to get drinks on the cuff.

Nearing a point where the upward-winding road started curving, the horse under him slowed, ears erect and forward tilted.

Twenty rods beyond the curve Amherst huddled behind the upthrust of rock, carbine gripped tightly, anxiously. Something warm rolled into the dark growth under his taped nose. He ignored it, but it was getting difficult to disregard the throbbing that drummed across his forehead and through his head. He sniffed and almost gagged when his plugged nostrils refused to take in air.

The heat against his back grew more intense, his right hand and the finger hooked around the Winchester's trigger were starting to cramp. He waited a few minutes longer before it dawned on him that something wasn't right. Slowly he drew back, started to push himself upright yelping, spilling frantically on to his side when a slug whined off rock close at his left.

'Drop it!' a voice snapped when Amherst rolled on to his back, trying to raise the gun into a firing position. Another shot sent rock fragments nicking into the side of his neck. He flung away the rifle, held his hands where they could be seen.

Ordered to do so,, he rose clumsily, hands kept at shoulder level. 'How the hell. . . ?' He stared at

Rourke standing a few yards away. Using the back of his hand, he made a careful swipe at his nose, swearing softly at sight of the streak of blood.

'Took too long,' Rourke told him. 'Spotted you from the bottom. Figured we should've passed each other about halfway.' A shrug dismissed the rest. 'Now, you got a name, spit it out.'

'Amherst,' came the reluctant reply.

'Ballentine's crew?'

It was slow in coming, the curt nod, the muttered, 'Yeah.'

'Whose idea?' Getting no immediate answer, Rourke thumbed back the Colt's hammer. 'Last time.'

'Nobody's!' Amherst blurted sullenly. 'It just came to me.' He made another gentle wipe at his nose, held out his hand to show the red smear. 'On account of this. Damnit – you had it comin'!'

'Pay back with interest don't you?' Rourke returned quietly. 'You're the one followed me out of the saloon. That also your idea? Or Noonan's?'

Again there was no answer, but none was necessary.

'One more question, and this time don't keep me waiting. Where'll I find Tobin?'

'Tobin?' The expression that wrinkled Amherst's face was more eloquent than his words. 'I don't know no Tobin.'

'Smart thing to do,' Rourke said, 'would be to put a bullet through you, make sure you don't try anything like this again.' He motioned with the gun. 'Unbuckle, then drift.'

Amherst stared back without understanding.

Impatiently, the gun made another gesture. 'Move – before I change my mind.'

The Diamond B rider waited no more. Shedding belt and holster, he looked again at Rourke to make sure this was not some trick. Then, with a quick nod that could have meant anything, took off to where he'd left his horse.

Ollie Kramer, skinny and stooped, with the face of one who'd been fed a jug of vinegar, performed another appraisal of the roan's owner when taking the reins handed him, mud-coloured eyes thinned shrewdly.

'Sheriff's been lookin' for you.'

'That right?'

Kramer's head bobbed and he came as close as he probably ever would to smiling. 'Was me, I'd go see what's on his mind.'

'Might do that,' Rourke said in easy agreement, but from the stable steered himself onward to the hotel.

A half-hour later, stripped to the waist, he finished towelling down, reached for the clean shirt, and caught his reflection in the mirror. Along his ribs the bruises had turned almost black, but he could live with them. For a longer while he studied the scar across his chest. . . .

They'd been lucky to find such a protected place to make camp. The day had been long and rough, culminating in rain and howling, biting wind, but neither he or Wally had minded. Close on two years of back-breaking work, of living only slightly better than savages, was behind them; within just a few more days papers would be signed that would finally make them legal landowners.

He'd slept the sleep of the dead that night, hearing nothing until gunshots jolted him back to life.

For one brief moment time appeared to stand still and, in the light of a dying fire, he saw Wally's empty blankets and heard himself yelling his partner's name while grabbing up his holstered gun. Before he was fully erect a shadowy figure was rushing from where the horses were picketed, pointing a gun that belched fire and knocked him backward and into oblivion.

When his eyes opened it was to the sound of a bird calling from a distance, being answered by another even further away. Red streaked a slowly brightening sky and all around was the funereal smell of damp earth. At first there was only confusion, no clear memory of anything. Then, like a lamp being suddenly turned up, everything came back in a flood of recall. He tried to raise himself, but the pain in his chest pinned him to the ground. He called to Wally, and got back only silence. He felt the front of his shirt, the stickiness that seemed to be everywhere. A brassy dryness lined the inside of his mouth and his throat burned. He tried again to lift himself but, unable to find the power to do so, lay where he was while nausea churned up his gut.

There came a hazy, quickly vanishing recollection of someone leaning over him, breathing heavily. Disregarding pain and all else, with a strangled groan he somewhere found the strength to get himself into a sitting position, to fumble at his waist.

The money-belt and the three thousand that would be the last of what they needed to bind the deal, was gone.

Rourke pulled on the shirt, buttoning it as he turned to the cheap bureau on which he'd placed a few personal items. From these he took what used to be a very fine gold-plated watch. Never again would it keep time, for a chunk of lead had smashed and reshaped it beyond repair. He put it in the left pocket of his shirt where always it had been carried. As a watch it was useless, but he clung to it because once it had been his father's, and once it had saved his life.

He was still straightening up, still half-turned, when that yellow-livered backshooter fired. The first shot missed but the second had struck the watch, twisted and torn it out of shape and sent it skidding and tearing across his chest. The impact had knocked him out, lost him a lot of blood – but he'd lived.

He had no idea how long it was before he was able to stand up, how he'd got to where Wally lay. Nor, after finding all three horses gone, how long he'd stayed in the camp, living on what few provisions had been left behind. All he knew was that it had taken a very long time, working and resting at short intervals, before he was able to get his friend buried. Wally Hatton, on the threshold of his fifty-seventh year, dead. And along with him all their plans.

But now, with each handful of earth dug, with each stone used to protect the grave, a new plan, a new intent, gained strength.

Sometime later he'd started walking, eventually landing up more dead than alive in a place called Astoria. It had taken a while, much longer than he could later believe, before he was able to get back on his feet and start his search along a trail long turned cold.

He reached for his comb, dragged it through his hair, and winced sharply. The ache was gone but there remained two bumps at the side of his head, both painful to the touch. Hardly was he through when knuckles rapped loudly against wood. He called for whoever was there to enter, and when Burrell stepped into the room it was to find himself greeted by the traffic end of a long-barrelled Colt. The sheriff frowned, came on in and shut the door behind him.

'Expecting trouble?'

Instead of answering. Rourke slipped the gun back into the rig he was holding, and buckled it around his waist.

Burrell went on, taking a grip on the lapels of his dark coat in a manner that made him appear even larger. 'Where've you been this time? The Diamond?'

'What you expected, isn't it? – why were you out there last night?'

Burrell let it pass. 'And?'

'Claim they never heard of any Tobin.'

'Said you'd be wasting your time.' Burrell dropped his hands. 'So what now?'

'Go on looking, I guess.'

'Riding on, you mean?'

'Meaning I go on looking till I find him. Occurs to me Tobin may just have been a name he was using for a while.'

Burrell let out his breath. 'Your time to waste any way you see fit,' he said, tone hardening. 'Just quit making a nuisance of yourself around the Ballentines. Miss Alecia's to be married soon and the last thing they need right now is someone like you making trouble.' Button eyes moved to the bruise on Rourke's face. 'Had some of it yourself, it seems.'

Rourke let a shrug be his only comment.

'One of the Diamond's riders was in town earlier,' Burrell went on slowly. 'Man named Amherst. You and him acquainted?'

'In a mild sort of way,' Rourke admitted, not bothering to mention their most recent encounter.

Burrell nodded. 'Kind of how I figured it might be.' He stepped back to the door and with a big hand wrapped around the knob, paused to deliver a parting shot. 'There's nothing for you here. So do yourself a favour – do us all a favour. Keep moving. This's peaceful country; we don't need the kind of trouble you could create.'

'Same's those folks I met up with this afternoon?'

Burrell's moon face went vacant. 'Who you talking about?'

'Family named Kieffer. Came to homestead and found themselves being made to feel anything but welcome – or safe. So they were packing up, getting ready to move on, like others before them. Leastways, that's how they told it.' Rourke's bronzed forehead revealed a couple of shallow lines when his head tilted. 'Strikes me you've already got trouble here, Sheriff. The kind that usually gets a lot worse before it gets any better.'

Burrell opened the door. 'Exactly who the hell are you?'

'That territory's already been covered,' Rourke answered.

The saloon had a slightly better crowd than the previous night. It also had a drunk on the verge of becoming dangerous: a stocky puncher, with a dark brooding face, whining bitterly about being unfairly kicked out of a job. He yelled for another drink, but the bartender shook his head. 'You've had more than your fill. You're also running out of coin. Save what you got for tomorrow.'

From where he stood at the end of the long bar,

Rourke watched the drunk clumsily haul out his gun, slam it down on the wood, and fling a slurred threat at the barkeep.

Rourke shuttled a glance toward the entrance. A few minutes past, responding to a signal from the bar, one of the Phoenix's customers had quietly departed, presumably to fetch some law. It was a situation similar to several in which he'd been directly involved, and, wanting no part in this one, he finished his beer and started for the doors which swung quietly open before he was halfway to them.

Manny Ebson hesitated only long enough to pick out his man before drawing his gun and striding forward, passing Rourke but giving no indication of having noticed him.

As he'd done the night before, Rourke stopped at the edge of the planked walk to roll up a smoke. This time, though, he was thinking of Ellen Terry, wishing he had some valid reason to call on her.

Back in the saloon there erupted sounds of a scuffle, a chair or table overturning, someone shouting and swearing. Just before the batwings crashed open the cursing became howling protestations. Ebson, holding on to the drunk by the back of his belt, shoved him on to the sidewalk.

Rourke stepped aside to get out of their way at almost the exact moment a pistol shot cracked across the relative silence of the street. The drunk let out a howl when suddenly freed from the deputy's grasp and was sent sprawling head first off the walk. From Ebson came a stunned gasp.

Mouth agape, he was standing very still, the hand holding the gun dropping, the other reaching to his chest. Rourke needed only a fast glance at the deputy to understand. Wheeling swiftly, he dropped into a crouch, ripping his own gun from leather, waiting for the next shot.

His eyes swept the other side of the street, over windows, doorways and entrances to alleys, and found nothing. He waited a few more seconds, ears straining towards the fugitive pounding of hoofbeats.

In the process, the drunk picked himself up and took off.

EIGHT

Burrell came out of the doctor's house to find Rourke waiting for him on the porch. Wordlessly they aimed for the street and only when closing the gate in the white-washed fence did Burrell say, 'He didn't make it. Doc got the bullet out, but it'd already done too much damage.'

They continued back into town, neither saying anything until arriving at the Phoenix where Burrell stopped, his gaze scouring the area in front of the swing-doors. Heaving slowly about he shifted his scrutiny to the buildings opposite the saloon.

'Still claim you saw nothing?'

Rourke answered with a slow shake of his head. 'Heard hoofbeats, that's all. Like someone anxious to make distance.'

'Always said that boy was inviting a bullet,' Burrell muttered, thumb and forefinger worrying his lower lip. 'Just never figured it this way.'

'Maybe,' Rourke said quietly, thinking of the afternoon's attempt by Amherst 'it wasn't him meant to get it.'

Burrell came slowly around. 'Go on.'

'If it was, wouldn't it have made more sense to wait until he was in better view?'

'You telling me something, or just making echoes?'

'Your choice.' Rourke went to the spot he'd occupied earlier. 'Here's where I was when Ebson and the drunk came barrelling through the door. I moved to get out of their way, which's when the shot was fired.'

'Missed you and hit Manny. That what you're saying?'

Rourke shrugged.

'So,' Burrell snorted, 'it's back to this Tobin character.'

'Uh-huh. Right back.'

While they stood outside the saloon, Jeff Ballentine was occupying a chair in the living-room of the house where earlier Rourke had thought of being. On a nearby brocade couch Ellen Terry waited impassively when he broke off in mid-sentence to make another fleeting assessment of his surroundings. The furnishings were good, the lamps elegant, the framed paintings tastefully selected, but in nothing could Ballentine find anything worthy of admiration.

'This's not for you, Ellen,' he went on, again facing her.

'It was never intended to be,' she said coolly. 'After my father was murdered it was thrust upon us – my mother and me.'

Ballentine adjusted his position in the chair, forcing down the annoyance that surged through him. 'I know,' he muttered. 'It was an unfortunate—'

Ellen stood up, a tightness in her tone when she said, 'Very unfortunate – being forced to sell, to buy this place. Unfortunate also that my father's killer has never been apprehended.'

Ballentine rose awkwardly. 'Ellen, I'm sorry. You know that. We tried to help. We paid your mother a good price for the JT, more than she'd have got from anyone else.'

'But still a rock-bottom price. Especially since your family had the most to gain.'

Ballentine began a reply, killed it and in a milder, almost pleading tone, changed tracks. 'Ellen, that's all past. Your mother's gone and you're alone. This isn't for you – you don't have to stay with it. At the Diamond I'd see that you got everything you—'

'And what,' Ellen cut in quietly, 'would Alecia have to say about that?'

'The blazes with Alecia,' he retorted hotly, 'I don't need her permission to marry you!'

'Let's not get into that again,' she said, crossing the room. 'It's been a long day, it's late, and I'm tired.' At the door she lifted his hat from the rack, holding it in readiness for his departure.

Ballentine's cheeks roaned up as he strutted stiffly to her and took the hat, jaw clamped tightly shut until she had the door open. 'Will you at least consider my offer?'

'It's late, Jeff,' she reminded him.

This time he had greater difficulty keeping a damper on his anger. 'One more thing,' he said gruffly. 'Presently there's a man called Rourke in town. If he should come here looking for accommodation, turn him away. He's not someone you'd want in your house. For that matter, anywhere near you.'

Ellen's brows lifted. 'That's an odd thing to hear! Personally, I've thought the gentleman to be considerate and—'

'You've – already met him?'

'As a matter of fact, I have.'

At the sides of Ballentine's jaw the muscles hardened and bulged. 'Keep away from him, Ellen. He – he's trouble.'

Pretending to think about it, she asked, 'Is that why your men attacked him? Because he's trouble? Trouble to whom, Jeff?'

Confusion narrowed Ballentine's eyes. 'My men?'

'Your men. That awful Charley Noonan and a couple of others.' She offered him a smaller frown. 'Are you saying you don't know about it?'

Storm clouds already sailing across Ballentine's long face became even more ominous when remembering the bruise on Rourke's face, the taped nose of Dave Amherst, explained away as just another saloon disagreement. He said, 'I don't. You have my word, I know nothing about it.'

'If you say so, ' Ellen Terry said, and opened the door.

Rourke reached the bottom of the stairs and heard his name called. Turning towards the hotel desk he saw the small, bespectacled owner nervously signalling him over.

'Mr-Mr Rourke,' Harvey stammered. 'I'm afraid I–I'll have to have your room.' A pale tongue flicked at his lips and he swallowed hard. 'I hope you'll understand.'

'I don't,' Rourke said, and waited for an explanation.

Harvey swallowed again, while behind perfectly round lenses watery eyes flicked fearfully to a point at the rear of the lobby. Rourke turned himself towards the dining-room, pushed open the glass-panelled double doors and ran his gaze over those already in for breakfast. At a corner table providing maximum privacy he located a face he knew.

Ballentine showed no surprise, offered no greeting when the tall figure loomed up before him.

'You own this place?' Rourke asked flatly.

'No, not that it's any of your business. Why?'

'Thought you might know why there's a sudden need for the room I've been occupying.'

'How would I?' Ballentine shrugged.

Hooking out a chair, Rourke lowered himself into it. 'Neither, I guess, would you know anything about one of your hands, a hairpin with a busted nose, trying to dry-gulch me?'

Very slowly Jeff Ballentine disposed of his knife and fork. 'That some kind of accusation?'

'At the moment, just a question.'

'And I'll answer same as before.'

'How about last night's business?'

'If you're talking about that deputy getting plugged – I heard. It's all over town. Tough break.'

'Might be,' Rourke said slowly. 'Especially if he happened to walk into a shot aimed at someone else.'

'Mister,' Ballentine said, retrieving his fork to spear at a small portion of ham, 'you're spoiling my breakfast. You got something to say, say it. And make it fast.'

'All right; I think the bullet was meant for me.'

This time there was a small clatter when Ballentine ditched the fork, sparks in his eyes when he put them on Rourke. 'You accusing Amherst? You saying it was him who—?'

Rourke slid back the chair and pushed upright. 'No. I don't think he'd be so stupid as to try again. Not so soon after bungling his first attempt.'

'Then who, damnit?'

'Tobin. Or whatever name he's presently using.'

'You're out of your mind!' Ballentine hissed.

'A possibility. Just the same, I think I'll hold on to the notion.'

Ballentine's lips moved stiffly, framing a retort, but before he had a grip on the words he was staring at Rourke's back, watching him push through the dining-room doors. Uttering a silent curse, he made an attempt to finish eating, but what still remained on his plate was cold, tasting as if it had been fried in axle grease.

At the stable Rourke found the roan saddled and waiting at the rack left of the broad front door. He went in, called to Kramer, and had to call again before a head popped up from behind one of the wooden partitions. Seeing who waited at the door Kramer's expression turned even more acerbic.

'Comin'! I'm comin'!'

When finally he did he was already talking. 'Had to put your horse outside. Be needin' all the stalls right soon.'

'Kind of expected you'd be,' Rourke said, fishing a half-dollar from his pocket, flipping it towards the stable man. 'That cover it?'

Kramer missed the catch and had to pick the coin up from the dirt. Anger lifted his stooped shoulders when he straightened; he started to say something, thought better of it and wheeled stiffly away.

Rourke had a foot in the stirrup when a buggy pulled up at the stable entrance. The broad figure of Doc Sturrett climbed heavily to the ground, called a tired greeting and started over.

'How's the head?'

'Almost like new.'

'Good, good.' Sturrett nodded, but his mind appeared to be elsewhere, his mood sombre. 'Wish the same could be said about young Ebson.' He cleared his throat, swung his gaze to the roan. 'Off somewhere?'

'Guess so. Seems both the hotel and the stable's needing all the space they've got.'

Sturrett turned sharply and Kramer was too slow to step out of the doorway where he'd been lurking and listening. 'What's this? When last was your place completely full?'

Kramer faded back into the building without answering.

'What's going on?' Sturrett wanted to know.

'Not sure, Doc. Seems certain parties would prefer to see me gone.'

Sturrett removed his hat to run fingers through thinning grey hair. 'Try never to poke my nose into the business of others. Way I see it, if folks want me to know something they'll tell me.'

'I'm looking for someone,' Rourke told him. 'Man who once called himself Tobin. Few killings he needs to answer for.'

Sturrett replaced his hat. 'Never noticed any badge when I checked you over.'

'None to be found. This's personal.' Before he'd finished Rourke could almost hear the thoughts clanging around in the medico's head.

Eyes weighing the taller man, Sturrett heaved a weary sigh. 'This is where I go back on my policy. This search you're on . . . it got anything to do with that scar across your chest?'

The other smiled remotely. 'Uh-huh.'

For a handful of seconds Sturrett went on squinting speculatively. 'Kramer's lying, of course, and I'd

imagine old Harvey had reasons for feeding you his
load of bulfalo-chips. Someone gave them instructions, and there's only one man I know of who wields
that kind of power.'

'Ever think of trading your bag for a Pinkerton
badge?' Rourke asked, still smiling.

A big hand waved away the suggestion. 'Didn't
take much to figure that one out. Had an early call
this morning. Saw his horse stabled here when I
came to get my buggy. Also know the family have two
rooms on the top floor of the hotel, permanently
reserved for when they stay over in town.' Sturrett
nodded thoughtfully. 'All of which makes for some
interesting conjecture.' Then another thought
struck home. 'One more question,' he said, even
more gravely, 'and I won't bother apologizing for it.
What happened to Manny Ebson – it somehow
connected?'

Rourke stalled his reply for a moment, then gave a
slow nod. 'It's my opinion, but it's a lonely one.'

Of a sudden Sturrett was all business, hauling his
bulk to its full height. 'And you're riding away from
it?'

'No.'

'Then where are you going to stay?' Giving Rourke
no chance to answer, he said, 'I could put you up, if
you can stand the inconvenience of regular inter-
ruptions.'

'Thanks, Doc, but I don't want to cause you any
trouble.'

Sturrett's reply was loaded with derision. 'That's
the last thing that bothers me. I'm the only doctor
this town's got – hell, the only one in twenty square
miles. They'd think long and hard before messing
with me.'

Rourke studied the broad, stern face. 'You know nothing about me. Not where I come from or what I've been. Why'd you want to stick your neck out?'

'From where I'm standing it looks like you're about to go up against the Ballentines, which is reason enough. There's a family that's walked mighty proud – and over too many people in the process. There's also the fact,' he continued less harshly, 'that young Ellen Terry appears to trust you enough to go to your aid.'

Rourke started to speak but Sturrett snapped his fingers and shook his head disgustedly. 'For sure I'm getting old. Here I am, talking about the lass, and completely forgetting the business she's running. You might get a room there.'

'Thanks, but I'd as soon avoid bringing any of my problems to her door. Fact is, I've got a place in mind.'

'Pity,' Sturrett mused, 'because that'd really put Ballentine's nose out of joint.'

NINE

An hour before noon Ballentine arrived back at the Diamond in time to find Maurie Kortman on his way out. He hauled up beside him.

'What are you back here for?'

'Needed something,' the lanky ramrod answered with deliberate vagueness, not liking the suspicion echoing in the question.

Sensing the resentment, Ballentine pressed no further. 'Where've you got Vance and Dwyer?' he asked instead.

'*I* got 'em no place,' Kortman scowled. 'Said they was to take orders from you direct, didn't you?' Seeing Ballentine's expression harden, he nodded towards the bunkhouse. 'Back there.' Then: 'Why'd you send for them, Jeff? We don't need their kind to hold on to the flats.'

'Realized that,' Ballentine grunted, nudging his mount onward across the yard. 'Which's why they'll be leaving.'

The strongest of the odours permeating the bunkhouse were those of whiskey and stale cigarette smoke. Ballentine went on in, stopping at the board table in the middle of the long room, glowering at the empty bottle, the scatter of playing-cards and litter of cigarette-butts. Grabbing the bottle, he moved on to the very end bunks where both Vance and Dwyer lay stretched out on their backs. Dwyer, his open mouth exposing tobacco-stained teeth, snored quietly, erratically. Vance watched from behind lowered eyelids.

Ballentine waited. 'This the time of day to be sleeping?' he growled irritably when still neither man stirred.

Leisurely, Jesse Vance sat up, swinging his legs to the floor, a dead smile on his gaunt, pock-marked face. 'Said to hang around, didn't you?'

Dwyer yawned widely, shifting his small, wiry frame into a sitting position. 'What th' hell else is there to do around here?'

'Not this!' Ballentine said fiercely, showing them what he held. He flung the bottle away, not caring where it might land.

'Whoo-ee,' Dwyer grinned, his short blade of a nose flattening out when he did. 'Comes on strong, don't he?'

'Shut up, Burt.' Vance rose to his feet. A narrow-shouldered man with straight black hair and a small slash for a mouth, his eyes levelled with Jeff's. 'I think Mr Ballentine's 'bout ready to tell us the work bell's just rung.'

For a while Ballentine was silent. Then he shook his head. 'Gather up your gear. You're moving out.'

Vance and Dwyer waited for the rest, displaying neither surprise nor curiosity.

'Things have changed,' Ballentine said. 'The kind of work I had lined up for you – it's no longer necessary.'

'Just like that,' sneered Dwyer. 'You bring us here—'

'Shut up,' said Vance. 'Let him finish.'

'You'll get two months' pay for your trouble,' Ballentine informed them. 'But you're clearing out today. Any objections?'

'Hell, no,' Vance grinned. 'Just so long's we're gettin' paid. Then again,' he went on, thoughtfully massaging his jaw, 'me and Burt, we been givin' the deal some consideration of our own, and what we concluded is that maybe we hired out too cheap.'

Ballentine's lips twisted. 'You'll get no more than what was agreed. But' – and suddenly, though his eyes retained a savage intent, his face smoothed out – 'I've got another job in mind. Handle it right and there'll be ten double eagles coming your way.'

Dwyer, lifted himself upright, pale eyes narrowing. 'Each?'

Ballentine's immediate impulse was to belt the smaller man, but then it was as if he was listening to an echo of Alecia's warning. Reluctantly he nodded. 'All right. Each.'

Vance laughed softly. 'But first we got to clear out, right? So if things go sour we're no longer connected. That what this's all about?'

'If you're as good as you claim,' Ballentine returned grittily, 'nothing will sour. But if it does—'

'We're on our own,' Vance finished.

'Well?'

Vance shrugged. 'So what's the party's name?'

'And how about,' Dwyer grinned, 'we see some of that cash in advance?'

Watching the grin stretch insolently across the man's face, Ballentine wondered if Kortman was right, that it had been a mistake sending for this pair.

Suddenly it felt as if there'd been a slight but meaningful shift of control.

Alecia was in the kitchen with the Mexican woman who cooked and kept house for them, when Ballentine stalked in. 'Where's Howie?' he demanded.

Alecia's response was a quick, cutting glance, and only when through with the cook did she give him her full attention. 'In the parlour,' she ordered imperiously.

Ballentine followed her to the huge front room where she turned angrily upon him. 'How many times do I have to tell you not to discuss family matters in front of the help?'

'Where's Howie?' he repeated.

'I've no idea,' she returned coolly, annoyed that her reprimand had been brushed aside. 'I've barely seen him. He got in late last night and was gone again early this morning.'

'Gone where?'

Alecia shrugged delicately. 'I had no opportunity to ask.'

Ballentine gave a disgusted snort. 'When he gets back, tell him I want to see him. Tell him to stay here until I do! Otherwise – otherwise—'

'Otherwise?' Alecia's coolness gave way to swift concern.

'Otherwise I'll break his damned neck!' her brother snapped, walking heavily away.

'Those new men,' she said quickly. 'I saw them leaving . . .'

Jeff heeled slowly about. 'You wanted to be rid of Rourke, didn't you?' he asked, trying to match her earlier calm.

*

Heavy, low-sailing clouds were robbing the afternoon of some of its already fading light, doing nothing to improve Les Mayo's mood. 'Damnit,' he complained, 'he could've thought of this earlier. Now we'll be late gettin' back for chow.'

Riding at his side, Charley Noonan tossed him a taunting smile. 'Shoulda told him so when you had the chance.'

'Ah, shut up,' Mayo growled, his prematurely aged face tightening up. Gingerly he fingered his scabbed lip. 'Far's Kortman's concerned, you're no different to the rest of us.'

'Just got more sense,' Noonan returned. 'I take my pay and do like I'm told. Like that everybody stays happy.'

'Pity you didn't think that way before gettin' me and Dave to help you lay for that—' He broke off, swinging his gaze sideways. 'Hell, you didn't even know the jigger's name when you sicced us on to him.'

'Know it now,' Noonan nodded meaningfully.

'Be easy you said,' Mayo went on, fingers again at his injured lip. 'The hell it was! I wind up with this, and Dave's got a busted nose. You got off clean.'

'There'll be another time.'

'Not for me there won't. You heard what happened last night – the tellin'-off me and Dave got from Kortman! Hell, he's lucky he's still got a job.'

Noonan gave him a hard look. 'Don't lay that on me. I never told him to go gunnin' for nobody. He brought that on himself.'

Mayo gave no indication of having heard a word. Instead he gigged his mount to a faster pace. 'C'mon. Let's get this over with so's we can get back.'

When they came to a halt it was at a small, timber

cabin, backed against a thin grove of pine, and a couple of roughly constructed sheds. There'd been a third which, judging from the spread of ashes and blackened timber, had been the largest. An air of desolation, made heavier by the grey of the afternoon, hung over everything. Fences which once surrounded sections of cultivated land were reduced to a tangle of wire and unpeeled poles. The earth itself looked as if a trail herd had been stampeded across it, churning up whatever had been planted, leaving the yield to rot.

Mayo cast another disapproving glance at the sky. 'How we goin' to do it?'

'You heard Kortman.'

Reluctantly Mayo climbed to the ground. 'Some coal oil would've helped,' he muttered with displeasure. 'Now we got to do it the hard way.' He looked up at his companion. 'Well? You just goin' to sit there on your fat rump?'

'Quiet,' Noonan growled, squinting into the distance.

Following his gaze, Mayo listened. 'Rider comin' . . .'

'An' from the sound, already pretty close.'

'There!' Mayo pointed. 'Comin' out on the left of that gully!'

A puzzled expression slid on to Noonan's round face. He stroked the heavy growth matting his upper lip. 'No sodbuster, that. Not the way he's ridin'.' He dropped his hand, loosening his holstered gun.

In silence they waited, both dismounted, listening as the muffled drumming grew louder, the image of the horseman larger, more distinct. He rode at an easy lope, right arm hanging loosely at his side, but not until he was almost fully upon them, reining the big blue to a walking halt was there any sign of recognition.

When it came, Charley Noonan swore sharply and grabbed for his gun. The rider's dangling arm lifted and a Colt's long barrel spat a sharp warning.

A soft, gurgling sound came from Les Mayo's throat.

Rourke gave him but a glance before lifting his eyes back to Noonan, who stood rooted. 'Something you wanted?'

Noonan's hand dropped away from his weapon. 'You know what's good for you, butt out. This's none of your business.'

'Wrong. When you and your pals jumped me, you became my business. Now you're trespassing, which makes it more of my business.'

'Trespassin'?' The word was a small eruption from the shorter, broader man's mouth. 'This's Ballentine land – part of the Diamond B!'

'Wrong. This's government land, and this section's been legally filed on by one Ryman Kieffer.'

'A stinkin' nester!' Noonan snarled.

'Careful,' Rourke warned. 'You're referring to a friend of mine. Reasons of – shall we say, family health? – forced him to leave for a while.'

This time Noonan made no interruption.

'Meanwhile, I'm watching over things. And like you've already been told, unless you have legitimate business, you're trespassing.' Rourke nodded toward the torn-down fences, the trampled earth, the gutted building. 'Diamond's doing?'

Noonan ignored the question. 'Mister,' he breathed harshly, 'you're buyin' into a whole mess of trouble. Nobody in this county bucks the Ballentines. And you're nobody! So get out of our way!'

Rourke gave an easy shrug. 'Feel that strongly about it . . .'

Mayo swallowed. 'Charley, forget it. Let's get out of here.'

Noonan's mouth shaped into a sneer. 'He don't scare me. We been told to torch this place, which's exactly what we're gonna do.'

He took a tentative step towards the cabin, braking sharply when Rourke's gun barked a second time and whipped the hat from his head. He spun round, cursing. Rourke swung out of saddle. For a handful of seconds before touching ground his back was to Noonan – who was fast to recognize opportunity. Like a lumbering bull, neck pulled into meaty shoulders, he charged.

Almost within reaching distance he realized too late that his quarry was turned – facing him and waiting. The Colt lifted, then arced down hard against the side of Noonan's skull, dropping him flat on his face.

Les Mayo stared. Slowly his eyes lifted to the man standing over Charley Noonan's inert bulk. 'You—' He swallowed, made another try. 'You did that deliberate! You suckered him!'

'Thought he was trying to collect something owed, is all.' Rourke stepped back. 'Load him up, then git.'

It took Mayo a while and all of his strength to get his partner to his feet. By then Noonan was already starting to come round, able to lend some help getting himself up into saddle. One hand fastened to the horn, he stared drunkenly down at the man who had buffaloed him.

'Keep riding. Don't even try to look back. And, you' – Rourke's gun singled out Mayo – 'tell Ballentine there'll be no more trouble from your outfit.'

His wizened face deadpan, Mayo nodded mutely. From Noonan came a weak, contemptuous snort. 'You don't know it, but you're already buzzard bait!' He started to turn his horse away, but Rourke's voice held him.

'Here's something else you can carry back. Tell Tobin I'm waiting.'

Mayo traded a puzzled glance with Noonan before turning a frown upon Rourke. 'Who's he?'

As they rode away, from the corner of his eye, Rourke sensed vague movement at his left. For only a moment, at the top of a rise almost a mile distant and hazy against the drab sky, he thought he'd seen a third horseman abruptly drop from sight.

By the time the two Diamond riders were no more than shrinking specks, a chill had settled across the flats. Rourke collected the roan's trailing reins and led him to a roughly constructed shelter attached to the rear of the cabin.

Which was when he noticed the tracks of another horse.

They were recent and could have been made by either Mayo's or Noonan's mount. Then he found the single bootprint – flat-heeled and faint. His gaze shifted back to where he had thought he'd seen a third rider and he thought of the old man who'd brought help after Noonan and his bunch had jumped him. The thing he still struggled to remember concerning Wally's killing made a lightning flash before his eyes, vanishing before he had a chance to grab at it. Shaking his head in frustration, he led the blue the rest of the way into the lean-to and began unsaddling.

He filled the narrow trough with hay from the small supply Kieffer had been good enough to leave behind, then hand-fed the roan from the bag of grain he'd included in the few supplies brought from town. When through he went to the broad box built up against the cabin wall, and lifted the lid. Inside was enough firewood and kindling to last a couple of days. A section of the cabin wall, equal to the width of the box, had been cut away, but the small stack of wood and the fading light made it impossible to see what was on the other side.

He was lowering the lid when the first drops of rain struck the roof of the lean-to, and within a matter of seconds darkness dumped itself down upon the land. He gave the roan's rump a friendly slap, started for the cabin's rear door – and was stopped in his tracks by a cold, feathery touch at the back of his neck. He swept back his coat, had his fingers already wrapped around the Colt when a shot blasted viciously across the yard.

The horse snorted, turning its head in time to see its owner pitch forward. It snorted again, but the sound brought no movement from the form upon the ground.

A long silence broken only by the gentle beat of the rain stretched itself across the yard, and still nothing stirred. Then, when it seemed as if nothing ever would, from somewhere in the clustered pine came the furtive scraping of boots slithering cautiously forward.

On the dampening ground Rourke's body remained inert.

The footsteps inched closer. Then, as if to be doubly sure, the pointing gun clenched tightly in the attacker's hand, stretched forward, finger tightening around trigger for a second shot.

A startled yell froze the intention when suddenly

the sprawled figure huddled upon the dampening earth rolled over and a crack of thunder sent a widening circle of fire hurtling through the night.

TEN

'So' – anger and disgust thickened Ballentine's voice as he stalked into the spacious front room – 'you've at last decided to spend some time at home!'

Slacked out on the couch, expensive boots propped up on a low table, Howie had both hands wrapped around a glass. Without looking up, he muttered, 'Leave me be, Jeff. I'm not in the mood.'

Ballentine stomped heavily all the way in, skirting the couch to hover over his younger brother. A big hand lashed out, swiping the drink from Howie's grasp, jolting his feet to the floor. 'This's a working ranch, squirt! You want to stay here, you want to eat – you do your share or get out!'

The unexpected sound and sharpness of his sister's voice brought Ballentine's head up with a jerk. His shoulders slumped. 'Come in, Sis. You need to hear this.'

Alecia closed the door behind her before moving soundlessly to where she was able to face both brothers. 'What on earth's going on between you two?'

Jeff chose not to hear the question, flinging instead one of his own at Howie. 'Where were you last night?'

White-faced, Howie shot to his feet. 'Since when do I have to account to you for everything I do?'

'Don't pull that one on me, squirt!' Ballentine fumed. 'I'll tell you where you were! In town – skulking in an alley like a mangey coyote, waiting your chance to put a bullet into Rourke!'

'You're crazy!' Howie swung toward his sister. 'Alecia – he's out of his head!'

'Shut up!' Ballentine bellowed. 'I'm sick to my gut of your lies! I'm not Ma – I'm not Alecia! They don't work on me!'

'Leave Ma out of this!' Abrupt fury put a shrill note into Howie's voice.

'All right,' Ballentine sighed, 'but just for once, try to be man enough to tell the truth.' His eyes flicked to Alecia's thin, bloodless face, then back to his bother. 'In case you haven't heard, your shot missed Rourke and hit Burrell's deputy instead.'

'Damnit,' Howie's voice remained high. 'I told you—'

'He's dead,' Ballentine went on. He reached forward, clamping both hands on Howie's shoulders, shaking him violently. 'Now, for once in your miserable life, let's have the truth!'

'Jeff,' Alecia broke in, 'what is this all about?'

'Ask him,' he answered tightly, shoving Howie away, watching him collapse back on to the couch.

Alecia turned to the boy. 'Howie. . . ?'

He swallowed hard. 'He – he's crazy! I – I don't know where he got all that stuff from. I never saw this Rourke in my life! Why'd I want to kill him?'

'Another lie!' Ballentine growled derisively. 'You saw him all right – the night you bust into his camp, the night you killed his partner and left him for dead! Maybe you don't remember what he looked like, but you remember his name!' His eyes clamped on Howie, holding him as if they were hooks of steel.

'Jeff,' Alecia said hoarsely, 'you're making no sense!'

Ballentine's gaze stayed fixed upon his straw-haired brother. 'I been thinking on it – hard – and finally it hit me. It's why Rourke's still around, why he's so damned convinced this Tobin or the one who used Tobin's name – is right here in Redemption.' He took a short step that brought him closer to Howie whose small body cringed back into the couch. 'Tell her how you knew who he was? Tell her!'

Howie shook his head, but when he spoke it was in a weak, defeated voice. 'You – you're crazy . . .'

'It was the moneybelt, wasn't it? The belt you stripped off him after you thought he was dead!' Ballentine let out his breath, eyes going to Alecia. 'The night Burrell came to tell us about Rourke, I saw the look on Howie's face when Rourke's name was mentioned.' His gaze returned to the boy, harsh and loathing. 'The belt – it had his name on it, didn't it? A name you weren't likely to ever forget!'

Howie Ballentine became perfectly still, all colour seeped from his face, leaving it shrunken and ashen. His mouth opened to begin another protest but before a single utterance was heard, lips began to tremble. Ever since he'd heard Burrell speak Rourke's name he'd been remembering looking down at a bearded face, hearing a groan from a man he'd thought already dead. After a while, in a voice that seemed to come from far away, from someone neither Alecia or Jeff Ballentine had ever known, he started to talk.

Out in the yard, Maurie Kortman was lighting a

freshly rolled smoke when he saw the two riders emerging through the near-dark.

'Where's Amherst?' he demanded when they stopped in front of him.

Noonan and Mayo traded quick, blank looks.

'Damnit I sent him after you – had a job the three of you could've done while still on the flats.' Then, realizing something was not right: 'What is it? You lugs run into trouble . . .'

'Yeah – kind of,' Noonan mumbled, refusing to look at the foreman.

Inside the house Jeff poured himself another stiff drink, trying hard to digest what Howie had revealed.

On the couch, in an effort to console him, Alecia had an arm wrapped around his narrow shoulders.

'It's your fault,' he whimpered. 'You told me to watch my step – refused to let me have any fun! If it wasn't for you none of it would've happened!'

Ballentine took a long swallow of the drink, contempt distorting his long face, narrowing smouldering eyes. The story Howie had just spun was of meeting up with Ken Tobin, down on his luck, with barely a dime to his name, of being told of Opulence, a town where the girls – particularly a certain little redhead – knew exactly how to take care of a man's needs. Tempted by the thought of the pleasures he'd expected to find at Golconda, and hadn't, Howie made a deal with Tobin – bought his horse and rig for a song, and that afternoon rode out of Golconda.

The rest was essentially as Rourke had told it. He'd woken to find the girl going through his pockets. Still a little drunk he'd flown into a rage – fleeing when believing he'd killed her, in his panic leaving his money scattered over the floor of the dingy room.

The hostler, sleeping off a drink when he'd taken

Tobin's horse from the stable, hadn't heard a thing. But it was only when racing aimlessly from the town, riding into foul weather, that he realized he was penniless. Again his story tied in with what Rourke had reported. Landing up in Astoria he'd broken into a store, killed the owner, and again panicked, leaving without a cent. Driving the horse mercilessly, he'd headed blindly into the hills where the weather was rapidly growing worse.

'When that fool animal slipped and went over the pass I – I was left stranded and freezing,' he whined. 'I thought I was going to die.'

'But you got lucky – stumbled into Rourke's camp, killed his partner—'

'Damnit!' Howie shouted. 'How was I to know he was moving away, had his back to me? It was dark! I thought he'd seen me, was going to shoot! I had no option.'

Ballentine had something to say, but a rap on the door, moments before it opened, brought him sharply around.

Alecia rose swiftly from the couch, flashing Maurie Kortman a furious glare, wondering how long he might have been listening on the other side of the door before knocking. Awkwardly, Kortman cleared his throat.

'Jeff, you'd better come outside.'

Outside, they found Noonan and Mayo dismounted, but still holding on to their mounts.

'Tell him,' Kortman ordered.

'I told you,' Noonan mumbled. 'He took us by surprise!'

'Damnit,' Jeff roared, 'stop wasting my time! You got something to say – let's have it!'

'Your friend Rourke,' Kortman said, when Mayo

and Noonan continued to stall, ' 'pears to've moved himself on to Kieffer's place.'

He glanced skyward as the first drops of rain began to fall.

Angrily, Tom Harding plucked the pipe from his mouth. 'Will you for Pete's sake quit that?'

'Sorry.' Spense halted his pacing at a window where an evening breeze played tag with the curtain. 'Got a lot on my mind.'

Harding crossed short outstretched legs, wishing the pain in his head would let up. 'Alecia?'

Spense hesitated, running fingers nervously through dark hair. 'We had words.'

From behind a thin plume of smoke Harding's ruddy face cracked into a slow grin. 'Bothering you that much, mosey on over and apologize. It's still early.'

For several long seconds Spense stared down at his father before slowly shaking his head. 'Pa, I don't know. This is all wrong. Calling it off might be the best – the right thing to do.'

'The hell it would!' Harding thundered, pain stabbing from temple to temple when he rose menacingly from the chair in which he'd been sprawled. 'A date's set and you'll go through with it even if I've got to hold a gun on you! You're not making a fool of that girl! Or of me!'

'Pa – I'm not even sure I really love her!'

A hand slashed the air as if to physically sweep aside the protest. 'You got the jitters, is all! It's only natural.'

'I – I don't know . . .' Spense took a short retreating step. 'This – this doesn't seem right.'

Tom Harding lurched forward, grabbing at his

son's shirt-front. 'You listen, boy,' he snarled, bulldog jaw rigid, 'and you listen good. You're marrying that girl! Hear me? You're marrying her just like it's been arranged, and I'll hear no more about it!' He released his grip and shoved Spense roughly away. 'Now get out of here! Go tell her you're sorry! Go on! Git!'

A sudden and completely alien fury blazed up within the younger Harding. He braced himself to stand up to his father but as fast as it had burst forth the emotion fizzled. Without another word he left the room.

Harding moved to the open window, got his pipe lighted again, and stood puffing on it, until he heard the slow clopping of hoofs. 'Damn fool boy!' he muttered, returning to his chair, wondering if a jolt of whiskey might case the ache behind his eyes.

A while later, his mouth was curved into a hard smile. When first Alecia had begun showing an interest in his son he'd encouraged it, every way possible. Even to the extent of going along with Jeff Ballentine's plans to rid the flats of the nesters. But that had not been a difficult decision.

Ballentine's arrogance continued to blind him to one important fact. He'd asked for no help from the other ranchers, only their moral support and none had offered more. When trouble developed – as it was bound to – it would be he, and he alone, the law would hold responsible. The Ballentines were the only ones who had anything to gain by holding on to Jacinto Flats.

He put down the pipe, folded his hands across his belly, and let the smile stretch wider as he thought about the rider who'd come to the Diamond. As he'd told them, the man was going to be a problem.

Exactly what sort of problem, he did not yet know. But he was trouble, this Rourke, the kind that could perhaps prove fatal to some ... perhaps fortuitous for others.

Closing his eyes, he let his imagination ride loose rein, oblivious to the hammering in his head. If Jeff Ballentine were removed from the picture, Alecia would inherit 'most everything. . . . As for Howie – as long as that kid had a few dollars to throw away at the tables in the Phoenix, he could be handled. The rest of the dream remained hazy. But of one thing he had no doubt: the time was rapidly approaching when at last he would get all he had been cheated out of by the man who'd called himself a friend.

He fetched a knife from his vest pocket, retrieved his pipe and set about scraping the bowl. Again he tried to determine exactly how Jake had managed the manoeuvre, and again he failed. But cheat him he had. Living so long in the shadow of Ballentine's success had thoroughly convinced Tom Harding of that.

Pretty soon, though, all would be put right, and it would start coming together right after Spense and Alecia tied the knot.

Even if he was forced to help matters along.

Harding's hands became motionless. For a long while he was perfectly still, remembering the story Rourke had told ... remembering Howie's reaction to Spense's question concerning Golconda ... the harsh glare Alecia had stabbed at his boy.

He sat upright. Of course! *That's* why she and Spense had fought! She'd confided in him – told him something she should not have! Very carefully he closed the knife and returned it to his pocket. He stood up, mind racing, and on unsteady feet went to the cabinet in which he kept a few bottles of branded whiskey.

He'd have to talk to Doc Sturrett about these headaches even if it meant getting glasses, like Spense had suggested.

'Jeff,' Alecia said censoriously, 'if you slowed down a bit on the whiskey and did some proper thinking—'

'What the blazes do you think I'm doing?' His gaze set firmly upon Howie. 'A fine mess you've made of everything! I thought we could handle the nester business without drawing attention from outside – but you've ruined that for us! You brought him here, you and your cursed stupidity!'

'Jeff!' Alecia sighed. 'Enough has been said on that subject! Howard made a mistake – a regrettable mistake that cannot be undone. But dwelling upon it isn't going to help matters one bit!'

Jeff slugged back the remains of his drink. 'Then supposing you come up with something, because, dear sister, I've a hunch Rourke knows a lot more than he's let on.' Eyes still pinning Howie to the couch, he asked: 'There something you still haven't told us?'

Howie shook his head.

Ballentine looked at his empty glass, then suddenly he was laughing, but without a trace of humour. 'Know something? If it wasn't so damn serious it could even be funny! To keep your name clean while whoring around, you use Tobin's – and while you're at it, for some cockeyed reason of his own, he's claiming to be working for us!' He turned to where the whiskey bottle waited, and stopped. 'I still think you're lying, holding something back.'

With a long withering sigh, Howie stretched to his feet. 'It's no use, Alecia! He'll never believe me. He never does.' Then, in a sudden, inexplicable surge of anger he swung back to Jeff. 'Remember, during the drought, when the Diamond was hurting – when we stood to lose a whole hell of a lot more than we could afford unless we got complete and clear access to the flats?'

Howie chuckled softly, enjoying the silence he'd established. 'There was only one solution left to you, wasn't there? Only it was a blocked trail. That is – until I went out and cleared it for you!'

Jeff's eyes narrowed. 'What are you yapping about?'

Alecia's face had become wraith-like. 'Howie,' she whispered, 'are you telling us it was you—' At the sound of quiet a commotion out in the yard she stopped abruptly to go quickly to the window. A moment later she was turned back to her brothers. 'Oh, my God – it's Spense!' She moved urgently to Ballentine. 'Jeff – please! I don't want him to know anything about this!'

Totally deadpan, Jeff left the room, pausing at the front door to grab a long canvas coat before stepping out into the soft falling rain.

In the yard Kortman and two hands gathered around a slicker-draped Spense Harding who stood between his own horse and one that had a body roped across the saddle.

'Found this on the way here,' he said when Ballentine joined them.

With the help of one of the hands Maurie Kortman untied the rope and eased the body to the ground, rolling it on to its back.

'Amherst,' he muttered, staring down at the taped nose. 'Got it twice in the chest, looks like.' He shook his head. 'Now what d'you suppose brought that on?'

ELEVEN

Before the first glimmer of light slid up from behind the misty ranges hulked along the eastern horizon, Rourke was awake, building a fire in the rough stone fireplace of the two-room cabin. Leaving water to boil for coffee, he went to take care of the roan.

Crisp and cold, the morning was so quiet the footfalls of a spectre would have been heard. Except for a few wispy clouds the sky had cleared, but in it remained nature's taunt of more rain.

He looked to where Amherst had fallen, wondering about the man. Either he'd been deliberately trailing behind Noonan and Mayo, or was on his way to join them. Maybe he'd seen what was happening at the cabin and grabbed at another opportunity to square accounts. Rourke quit trying to figure it, went back inside, and removed more firewood from the storage box.

A wide hole cut through the cabin wall connected it to the almost identical box he'd found in the lean-to, allowing for filling from the outside. It struck him as something Kieffer might have done simply to please or satisfy his wife. Like the other innovations:

the shelves and double bunks, roughly but imaginatively put together.

Restless and anxious to be moving, he fixed a simple breakfast, saddling up as soon as he was through eating. Other than knowing it would rile Ballentine – maybe force him into some reckless play that would expose the party who'd used the Tobin handle, who'd killed Wally Hatton – he was still unsure of his reason for electing to move on to Kieffer's place.

He rode aimlessly, stopping at two homesteads where he was greeted with caution, ill-concealed fear, and shotguns within close reach. At neither were the stories much different from the one heard from Kieffer, but when leaving he knew he'd failed to dispel their suspicions that he could well be a snooper in the Diamond's pay.

The sun had climbed considerably higher in the sky when he came to what so far appeared to be the only direct access to the flats, a point where the hills sloped sharply down to create a rocky, brush thickened pass less than a half-mile wide. Reaching the other side he followed a trail just wide enough for wagons to use, leaving it a while later to climb to the crest of a low, rock-cluttered hill. From there he could look down upon a narrow, slow-moving creek and the nearby run-down buildings of what appeared to have once been a ranch of some note. Leisurely he rolled a smoke, again wondering what had brought about the abandonment.

The cigarette was almost burnt down to his fingers when he saw the rider coming around the far side of a hummock of stunted pine, loping along at an easy, unhurried pace. Pinching out the smoke, he kept his gaze upon the horseman, and though the distance was still too great for identification, there was the feeling of knowing who it was that he watched.

Eventually the rider passed below, seemingly headed for the abandoned ranch. Rourke nudged the roan between the rocks screening him from view, heading a little way down-slope, gently pulling rein when the rider's head made a slight turn and from beneath a pale-coloured Stetson he saw a small flow of golden hair.

Thumbing his own hat back from his forehead he shook his head. Ellen Terry was the last person he'd expected to see astride a pony.

He continued to watch, admiring the manner in which she rode, like someone raised in a saddle. Then without warning, memories of Loretta ambushed his reverie. . . .

He was not yet twenty-one when his father died, leaving him heir to a thriving saddle- and gun-shop.

A bare three months later Loretta Videll became his wife.

Though only once had she bestowed her favours upon him, he'd believed her when she told him she was with child, allowed emotion and naïveté to surrender him to her tear-drenched pleas.

Had he heard any of the whispering and snickering, chances are he might have reached his thirty-first year less hardened, less bitter. But he'd not and before the second month of marriage was over, Tony Asche, a small-time faro dealer at one of the town's saloons, was not too subtly brought to his attention. Several times, while Loretta's young husband was at work, Asche had been observed leaving their home.

Instead of the hoped-for indignant denial when confronted about Asche, Loretta's response had been a smile that accused him of utter stupidity. Of course the child she carried was not his. Whatever had made him believe so?

Realizing he'd been duped, that everyone in town was probably laughing behind his back, Rourke reached for the bottle.

Late in the second month of pregnancy, his wife suffered a miscarriage, the cause of which she laid at his feet – an accusation her strait-laced parents were quick to accept. Three weeks later their daughter was packed and gone. So was Asche.

It was while shackled to the worst hangover he'd ever experienced that he received a visit from Ralph Patterson.

'I had no alternative,' the banker shrugged. 'You'd given her signing-power. I've tried to talk to you about it, but . . .' And after another uncomfortable shrug: 'Except for a few dollars, she's cleaned out your account.'

He'd sold the business, squared off debts, and bid the town goodbye, making no attempt to locate Loretta.

The next time he was truly conscious of anything was when waking up in a hotel room, feeling as if he'd died and gone to hell. That was two days after being tracked down by a detective working for a firm of San Francisco lawyers, and being served divorce papers. Loretta, he was a while later to learn, had dumped Asche and married a wealthy import-merchant.

Afterward there'd been neither hurt nor anger, no sense of loss. Whiskey appeared to have washed that all away, leaving only a deep sense of shame and self-disgust for allowing such a woman to turn him into what he'd become. He drifted and, probably because he still had little concern for the future, wound up as a hired gun in the middle of a bloody range war. Which was when he first discovered an unrealized proficiency with a Colt.

Shrugging aside the memories, he started down the hill. Almost at the bottom, still threading a path between massive boulders and thicket, he could see Ellen Terry riding the chunky little bay through the gateway, crossing the ranch yard to head directly for a tree-shaded knoll overlooking the creek. Then she was lost in the shadows.

He kneed the roan onward, but the going was slower now, his view of the ranch obliterated. When, a while later, he completed the descent it was in time to see two riders coming from the opposite direction from which the girl had arrived.

They passed under the timber arch, pointing themselves toward the main house – hauling up sharply when Ellen appeared at the yard's most distant end. Glances were exchanged, then they were moving again, pacing themselves so that they met up with her in the middle of the yard.

Curiosity chanelled shallow ridges across Rourke's forehead. For a while it looked as if the three were acquainted, but then Ellen was suddenly veering her pony away. One of the men grabbed the animal's headstall, hanging on while trying to snatch the reins away from her.

Scuffling hoofs, the girl's protests, the laughter of the man trying to drag her out of the saddle, kept them too busy to see or hear what was coming their way.

Until a shot slapped across the yard.

Instantly the one still trying to grab the girl reared away, twisting around, shouting as he clawed at his holster. His partner released his hold on the bay's cheek-strap, giving Ellen a chance to dig heels and send the horse leaping to freedom.

The shorter of the pair, lips stretched taut across tobacco-stained teeth got off the first return shot, letting loose a yell while the explosion was still echoing in his ears. The gun flew from his hand. Without letting the reins fall he clutched at his upper arm. He yelled again, using his uninjured left to jerk his mount around, racing for the protection offered beyond the buildings.

Pock-marked face a portrait of bitter surprise, his partner triggered wildly at the rapidly-approaching intruder. But under him the claybank was too skittish, ruining whatever chance he had of scoring a hit. He let loose one more shot, then, when lead tore a gash across the pommel of his saddle, skimming warmly across his thigh, he spun the animal about, leaning low across its withers as he sped after his companion.

By the time Rourke reached the rear of the buildings they were out of sight, hoofbeats fading among the low, timbered hills.

Ellen Terry was back in the yard when he returned, picking up her hat from where it had fallen during the skirmish.

He reined in beside her. 'You all right, Miss Terry?'

Lithely she swung back into leather. 'Thank you – yes.' Then, as if a little puzzled: 'I – I thought it was you, but I wasn't sure.'

Rourke nodded towards the direction in which the two men had retreated. 'And them?'

She shook her head. 'I've never seen them before.' Again the puzzled expression, this time accompanied by a small frown. 'But – they seemed to know you.'

'Then they have the edge.'

Ellen adjusted the hat on her blonde head. 'I'm sorry,' she said, offering a small smile of apology. 'That was an assumption. One of them – the one with the bad teeth – shouted a warning that made me think . . .' She paused, studying his sun-bronzed face. 'Actually, all he really said was – "It's him!" As I said, it was a silly assumption.' Her gaze shifted beyond Rourke, to the house. 'But what could they have wanted here. . . ?'

Previously, on the two occasions he'd seen her, she'd been dressed much the same as other town-dwelling women. Today, clad in a dark-brown split skirt lighter-coloured corduroy jacket, and half-boots, she was like a different person.

He said, 'Kind of surprised me to find you out here. More so to see you ride.'

She reached down to pat the bay's shoulder, to stop its restless pawing. 'This is where I was taught. The JT was once my home . . . before my father was killed.'

Rourke shuttled a glance toward the arch strad-dling the yard's entrance. Now he understood what the two letters burnt into the wood represented. A small frown asked his next question.

'While out riding, he was shot several times in the back,' she said softly. And then a little bitterly: 'Whoever killed him was never found – nor was any reason for his death ever established.'

'None of my business . . . but how come?' He gestured toward the abandoned buildings.

Ellen answered with a small rise and fall of her shoulders, turning from him to look back at the ancient cottonwoods on the shaded knoll.

'At the time the county was in the grip of a

drought. In over a year there'd been no rain. We were one of the more fortunate; we had a couple of springs that kept on supplying.' She sighed softly, facing him once again. 'But it was a difficult time for us without my father. He'd taken a note at the bank – one he'd easily have met, had he lived. But left alone . . .' She let a shrug finish the rest. 'The bank applied gentle pressure, but pressure none the less. My mother was eventually forced to sell.'

'To the Ballentines?'

She hesitated before answering. 'They were the only ones to make an offer – the only ones who could afford to.' Her head tilted up, and looking into her eyes he had a somewhat better understanding of the shadows that lurked there. 'Why am I telling you all this?' she asked quietly.

'Not sure, but I'm glad you felt you could.'

She went on looking at him. 'Who are you, Mr Rourke?'

'No more than what you see.' He shrugged. 'And the name's Jay.'

Giving no indication of having heard, she said, 'I was told you're in Redemption looking for someone.'

He held her gaze, watching disappointment wash slowly across her face when he failed to reply.

'Then you are what they say? A . . . gunman?'

'I wouldn't lie to you,' he answered. 'My gun's been for hire. But never for anything I need to be ashamed of. As for my reason for being here . . . Maybe some other time.'

She looked up at him again, her face now completely void of expression. 'Why not now?'

Rourke was silent, fearing just a little that if he told her it would put distance between them. But something in her voice seemed to reach deep into him and he heard himself saying, 'I had a good friend, name of Wally . . .'

Sickening of the range war, no longer sure if either side had any real justification for the continued fighting, he'd moved on, a long while later somehow wangling a job as shotgun messenger on a broken-down stage line. It wasn't much, but it gave him time to think, to quit feeling sorry for himself.

Afterwards, in several different towns, he was wearing tin, each day growing a little more remote. Then, as if the wheel was turning full circle, he was signed on with Wells Fargo, again riding shotgun. One morning he'd climbed up on to the box and found himself sitting next to an old-timer, a driver named Wally Hatton, a man with a dream he'd eventually shared.

There was a place in Wyoming Wally had seen, a place he'd like to sink roots – a good place for raising cattle or horses. 'Like a little piece of heaven come down to stay. Kind of place I think you'd cotton to,' he finished wistfully. 'Might even want to give it a look-over sometime.'

That such a venture could start in quite so casual a manner seemed impossible. Yet it had.

At first glance Rourke fell in love with the valley, but every cent he and Wally possessed had been only enough to purchase an option on the property. With three years given them to raise the price, it was Wally who'd come up with the notion of going into Utah to trap horses, selling them in surrounding territories where they were currently fetching top dollar.

Living on only the barest essentials, the days had been long, the work back-breaking, often brutal. The cost was high, but towards the end of the second year they'd stashed away enough to quit and head north, to sign the papers which would finally give them title to the land and buildings presently known as the Lazy J.

The three thousand in the moneybelt removed from Rourke's waist would have made it a reality.

Ellen was frowning deeply when he finished. 'The one who shot you – you know who he is?'

While he talked Rourke had been looking at the scuffle marks left on the ground, feeling as if they were trying to tell him something. He glanced up. 'Just his name – and now I'm no longer certain of even that.'

She went on frowning, but now with undisguised interest. 'And he . . . took all the money you and your partner had earned?'

Rourke smiled bleakly. 'Just the last three thousand needed to square the deal. The bank pass-book recording the bulk of our capital was wrapped in oilskin, sewn into the lining of my coat. He missed that. Not that it would've done him much good.'

His gaze dropped back to the beaten earth, still slightly damp from the previous night's rain. In it one of Ellen Terry's boots had left a fairly clear impression.

Suddenly he straightened, taking up the slack in the reins. 'If you've no objection, I'll ride back with you.'

Ellen smiled, and for a moment it seemed to Rourke as if a change had come to the blue of her eyes, as if some of the shadows had faded. 'Thank you,' she said. 'I – I'd like that.'

Rourke turned his head to look at the knoll she'd

visited, and she said, 'They're buried there – my mother and father.'

TWELVE

Jeff Ballentine slammed the door of the sheriff's office behind him, mutely cursing Burrell for digging up so many excuses in order to refuse his demands. From an inner pocket of his coat he produced a cigar, bit off the end and spat it out. He struck a light, glancing up sharply at two riders coming in from the far end of town.

His hand went still, dropping the match, all memory of what had happened in the sheriff's office submerged in a wave of frustration and blinding fury.

The riders turned off the wide street, leaving him with little doubt as to where they were headed. He flung away the unlit cigar, shoulders and neck rigid as he stepped off the boardwalk.

Rourke accompanied Ellen all the way home, offering to take her rented horse back to Kramer's stable.

During the ride back to town he'd received an answer to something which had puzzled him. He'd not asked, but Ellen had told him how, after Jack Terry's mysterious and unsolved death, after being forced to dispose of the JT, her mother bought the house on Coronado Street. Then, determined that her daughter should secure a higher education, she'd sent her off to a private school.

'It was Mother's hope that one day we'd be able to buy back the JT,' she'd told him. 'Which is why she started the boarding-house. It enabled her to save most of the money received for the ranch, and it brought in a reasonable income.' Her voice had softened, saddened a little. 'I knew that it would never happen . . . but I could never bring myself to tell her.'

Early in the third year of schooling Ellen returned from Boston to spend her vacation at home. Recognizing something amiss she'd talked to Dr James Sturrett and learned about the state of her mother's health. Then, despite strong opposition from her mother, she'd insisted upon staying home to help.

Five months later, on the shaded knoll at the JT, Lydia Terry was laid to rest beside her husband, and Ellen, not yet certain of what next to do, continued operating the boarding-house.

Along the way she suddenly pulled rein, turning to Rourke who rode at her right. 'I'm sorry. I – I can't recall when last I've talked so much. Especially about – about . . .'

He reached across, laid a hand gently upon her arm. 'Thanks. I'm proud it was me who got a chance to listen.'

Still at the office window from which he'd watched Ballentine stomp across the street, Burrell was not even aware of the rider dismounting at the hitch rack. For a long while he'd been concerned with the way events were shaping up, most of all Ballentine's increasing arrogance in his quest to expand that which his father had started, commencing to regard all connected with the Diamond above the law. He thought about the way his deputy had been shot down. . . .

Like a rat seeking escape, Burrell could feel the threat of trouble gnawing at his gut. It was time to start thinking of himself, his own future, before he was caught in the middle of something he couldn't stop.

The street door opened.

Rourke nodded a curt greeting, pulled back the left flap of his brush-jacket, carefully lifting a gun from behind his belt.

'Returning this in case someone reports it lost.'

Burrell came back to his desk, picked up the Army Colt, gave it a cursory examination. 'Where'd you find it?'

Rourke told him of the two he'd driven off the JT. 'Recognize them?'

'Never saw them before. Nor had Miss Terry. But they get in my way again, I think I'll know them.' He brought out tobacco and papers, began building a smoke. 'Had a look inside the house before leaving. Place's empty, but someone's been living there. Not long from the looks of things, maybe only a day or two.' He scratched a match against the leg of his jeans, lit the smoke. 'The JT – belongs to Ballentine now, right?'

'What of it?'

Rourke blew smoke, shrugged. 'Just wondering.'

'Been doing some of it myself,' Burrell returned stiffly, the gnawing in his stomach growing more intense. 'About a body roped to a horse that last night found its way back to the Diamond. Don't suppose you'd know anything about it?'

'Any reason I should?'

Burrell snorted derisively. 'Body belonged to one

of the Diamond riders, feller named Amherst. Recall you saying you and him were acquainted.'

'Uh-huh. Briefly.'

'Probably a little more than that I think.' Burrell paused, reaching uncertainly for a decision. 'Had Ballentine in here a while ago. He and two of his crew brought in Amherst's body. Was ready to swear out a warrant, claiming it was you who'd killed him.'

'His privilege,' Rourke shrugged. 'If he can make it stick.'

'Which is why I told him to drop it. But it doesn't mean he couldn't be right, and I got money says he is.' He paused again, this time allowing the silence to stretch. 'Heard you'd moved on to the Kieffer place.' Tiny eyes hardened. 'What the hell for?'

'Watching over it for him,' Rourke answered. 'Man got scared, afraid his two young girls would be hurt in the trouble he's been having, so he's moved away for a while.' He took a long draw on the quirly, let smoke stream from his nostrils. 'Had a little trouble myself. Couple of Ballentine's bully-boys came to torch the place, but they had a change of heart.' He leaned over to kill the cigarette in the sheriff's glass ash-tray. 'Which brings me to the other reason for being here. Far's I know, Ballentine's way out of line trying to run those grangers off land to which he's got no legal right. He continues, he's going to have the kind of trouble that'll swallow him whole.'

'From you?'

Again Rourke shrugged. 'It's the governor's office that'd give him his biggest problem, they get to hear what's going on.'

Long after he'd been left alone Burrell was still poised behind his desk. The moment he'd laid eyes on Rourke he'd recognized trouble, and now he was

being proved right. What worried him most was his
continued uncertainty – the possibility of the man
being more than he claimed. He was thinking, too,
of what Rourke had said the night Ebson was shot: of
the deputy getting in the way of a bullet that had his
name on it. . . .

Ellen was still in her riding-clothes when she
answered the door, surprised to find Jeff Ballentine
standing there.

Hat in hand, he greeted her sombrely. 'Mind if I
come in?'

'Jeff – it's not convenient right now. I've just got
back—'

'I know,' he said tersely. 'I saw you. And the person
I warned you about.' He sloshed the hat back on his
head. 'Why didn't you listen to me, Ellen? I told you
to keep away from him!'

Ellen's back went rigid. 'You – *told me*?'

'For your own good,' he amended hastily. 'You
know how I feel about you. I've asked you several
times to—'

'Jeff,' she cut in, her tone chilling, 'I have to ask
you something.' She waited, watching his face before
continuing. 'I was out at the JT this morning, putting
flowers on my parents' graves. Two men rode in –
tried to accost me.'

'*What*?' The sudden anger flaring in his eyes
shocked her.

'Nothing really serious happened,' she told him.
'Mr Rourke arrived before it could.'

'Rourke? What was he doing there?'

'Just – passing, I think. He drove them off.
Wounded one.'

'Those men – you got a good look at them?'

'No, not really. Everything happened too fast. All I know is that one had bad teeth, the other a badly pitted skin. Had Mr Rourke not been there . . .' The rest she left to his imagination.

Ballentine was silent, struggling to still the furies rampaging through him. At that moment he'd not have hesitated to kill three men, starting with Jesse Vance and Burt Dwyer.

'From the looks of things,' Ellen went on quietly, disturbed by the expression on his face, 'they'd been living at the JT – in the house.' She paused. 'Would you know why they were there?'

'Of course not! More than likely they were drifters, saddle-tramps,' he said huskily, jerking his hat tighter on to his head, wanting to be gone, yet unable to will his feet to movement. 'I'm sorry about what happened, Ellen but it's all the more reason why you should think about' – a hand gestured deprecatingly – 'giving this up, considering my offer.'

'Jeff,' she said quickly, with a quiet touch of resentment. 'I've a million things to do.'

A short distance from the house, almost invisible in the shadow of an oak's leafy overhang, a thin figure in a coat several sizes too big for him, watched Ellen close the door and Ballentine tramp back to where his horse was tied. Billy Deacon grinned, then sent a streak of tobacco juice into the dust. A while later he left the shadows, walking without haste to the brush at the end of the street, to where an old swayback wearing a mangey saddle waited. Once mounted, he rode up to the house, hoping Ellen might have something for him to do, something worth maybe two bits.

Maurie Kortman and Ben Yarbrough, a dark, hairy man, slouched at a small table in the Phoenix, wondering what was taking Ballentine so damned long. Yarbrough, who'd served the Ballentine family almost as long as the lanky ramrod, took a pull at his beer.

'Something 'bout that jigger botherin' you?'

Kortman pulled his slit-eyed gaze away from the man near the far end of the bar. He'd arrived ten minutes ago, showing no interest in their presence. Kortman started a reply, cutting it short when the batwings slammed open and Ballentine, face purpled with rage, steered a straight path across the room.

'Someone's sure as hell put a burr in his butt,' Yarbrough murmured.

Kortman motioned for silence, watching his boss knock down the drink in one swallow, wasting no time in tipping the bottle over the emptied glass. If he'd noticed either of his men he gave no sign of it; a reflection in the back-bar mirror had his complete attention. The second drink downed, he poured another before turning to stare down the length of the bar.

It was too early in the day for the saloon to have more than a handful of customers, and none stood between Ballentine and the man he faced.

'What the hell's still keeping you here?'

Meeting Ballentine's glare by way of the mirror, Rourke gave no response.

Ballentine stepped up closer, swallowed the third drink and got rid of the glass. 'I asked a question!'

Straightening and pivoting in one slow, easy movement Rourke pulled away from the mahogany. 'It troubles you?'

Ballentine's face set savagely. 'Damn right it does!'

'Pity, since I'll be around a while yet. Got business to finish.'

'You've got nothing to finish! The one you're hunting's not here – never was!'

'Think you're wrong – think I've got him tagged.' A flickering change swept across Ballentine's face, hardening his features, adding fuel to the blaze in his eyes. 'Was out at the JT this morning,' Rourke went on. 'Place Miss Terry tells me you now own.'

In three quick strides Ballentine was upon him, right shoulder dropping, lending all its force to the fist thrown at Rourke who was a little slow in getting out of its way.

The blow connected hard with the side of his head, knocking him sideways into a nearby table that toppled under his weight, dropping him to the floor. Ballentine moved in, hovering over him, fists knotted, teeth bared.

'Don't ever mention her name again! Don't let me hear you've been within a hundred yards of her, or so help me God I'll – I'll . . .' The rest ended in a splutter and a booted foot lashing out with vicious intent.

Slightly dazed, Rourke rolled up on to his feet, staggered a moment, but was ready when Ballentine spun around, fist cutting the air like a meaty cannonball. His left arm went up to block the blow and so violent was the impact he could hear the clash of connecting bone. The jolt of pain made him fear something had cracked. In that moment he knew Ballentine's bulk was a lot more than just shape, that the man packed power and, if allowed to gain the initial advantage, could cripple, if not kill him.

Pain still numbing his left arm, his right shot forward, crashing into the point of the heavier man's jutting chin, snapping his teeth together, sending his eyes rolling up in their sockets. He stumbled backwards, spat out a curse, and moved in to resume the attack. But, numbed though it was, Rourke's left was waiting. It smashed into his attacker's slight paunch, exploding air from his lungs, slamming him hard up against the bar. Ballentine bounced forward and a right hook caught him solidly behind the ear, driving him into the overturned table, tangling his legs.

Yarbrough and Kortman were on their feet but when Ballentine went to the floor and Yarbrough made to make the fight part of his own, Kortman grabbed his arm, shook his head.

Maurie Kortman had seen Jeff Ballentine in other fights, witnessed the brute force and savage strength of the man – seen him reduce others, bigger and heavier than Rourke, to whimpering, bleeding and broken bundles of flesh. Watching this fight, Kortman was aware of something else, an unleashed frenzy that had been triggered off by something Rourke had said. And Kortman, who had watched Jeff Ballentine grow to manhood, experienced no difficulty understanding why. Hell, Ballentine hadn't even mentioned them bringing in Amherst's body – trying to bring charges against Rourke. . . .

He saw Rourke's fist connect again with Ballentine's chin, and he winced, knowing that that which appeared to be the most threatening of his boss's features was in fact the place at which he was most vulnerable. It had always confused Kortman that, in spite of Ballentine's strength, of being able to take more punishment than any two normal men, he had never been able to ride a direct blow to the jaw.

Ballentine was in trouble and he knew it, but all it did was add to his rage. He swore again, pushing up on to hands and knees, shaking his head in an effort to clear it. His eyes stayed glassy.

'Enough?' Rourke asked, still a little surprised and

shaken by the realization that it was not his presence in Redemption, nor the shooting of one of the Diamond's crew that had provoked the sudden and almost insane attack, but the mere mention of Ellen Terry! The man was in love with her! With some pity he watched Ballentine struggle to his feet. 'Enough?' he asked again.

Ballentine's response was a thunderous roar of malice. He shoved upwards, blood trickling from the corner of his mouth, hand already jerking at the holstered gun, hanging slightly askew at his side. Rourke's numbed left stopped him when it thudded hard into his ribs, his right tilting up the thrust-out chin, rocking Ballentine backwards – and into the arms of Ben Yarbrough. At the same moment Rourke felt something poke hard into his side.

'It's over,' Kortman announced.

'The hell it is!' Ballentine shouted. 'Keep out of this Maurie! Yarbrough – let me be! I'm going to kill that dirty son-of-a-bitch!'

Rourke lifted his hands. 'Some other time. Like your man said, it's over. For now.' Ignoring Ballentine's continued struggles he picked up his hat, slapped it against his leg to get rid of the dust, and fitted it back on to his head.

Ballentine jerked free. 'Get out of town!' he hissed, wobbling, stepping backwards into Yarbrough. 'Get the hell and gone from Redemption! By sunrise tomorrow – be long gone! Or s'help me, you'll never see another one!'

Rourke shook his head. 'Sorry. Still got things to do.'

'Then,' Ballentine said through clenched teeth, 'I'm serving notice on you now. You murdered one of my men and I'll see you swing for it. You're still around tomorrow, you'll be wearing a price on your head!'

THIRTEEN

Word of the saloon fight reached Burrell within minutes, but he made no effort to investigate, fully expecting to have Ballentine again come storming into his office. Instead, from his window he watched the owner of the Diamond B, his ramrod, and the man called Yarbrough, leave the Phoenix and head for the offices of the *Redemption Register*.

What the hell business, he wondered, did they have there?

Still later, a while after Ballentine and his men had left town, he saw Rourke ride out, and the gnawing in his gut became almost unbearable.

Following Rourke's departure, another rider, a slim form on a sleek chestnut, moved out from one of the alleys, loping slowly along in Rourke's shadow. No one paid him much attention, and by then the sheriff was back at his desk.

In no hurry to return to the emptiness and gloom of the Kieffer cabin, Rourke detoured back to the JT. At the graves of Ellen's parents he lingered a while before wandering through the deserted buildings, and finally the big house itself. It told him little, especially of the two men he'd found there. But in some obscure manner he had a sense of how life had once been at the ranch – and how Ellen Terry felt about the loss.

Leaving what was left of the JT he brought the roan to a walk while he fashioned a smoke, casting another covert glance along his back trail. Since leaving town there'd been the feeling that someone trailed behind him, yet he could still find nothing to substantiate the notion, not so much as the smallest rise of dust.

He shrugged away the feeling, recalling Ballentine's threat to put a price on his head. Exactly what that meant, he wasn't sure except that, whatever it was, it spelled trouble. In his own mind it also confirmed that Ballentine knew who had been using the Tobin name at the time of the girl's death, who it was who had ambushed him and Wally, and that he was now aware that Rourke also knew.

The problem was how to prove it in a county where the Ballentines reigned supreme!

Shadows were thickening when he reached the broken ground through which the stream meandered within easy walking distance of the cabin. Again he gave thought to the time and cause of the upheaval of earth. The trail he moved along drifted between clusters of boulders, brush and stunted piñon, crossed through the slow-running water, and lifted up on to the flatlands on which Kieffer had settled – where, less than half a mile away, at least a hundred head of Diamond B cattle grazed.

They were about to cross the stream when the roan's ears twitched, its head jerking slightly to the left. But even as the animal's uneasiness touched Rourke there came the soft whistling of a rope sailing through the air before it dropped over his shoulders, pinned his arms to his sides, and jerked him violently from the saddle.

Les Mayo scrambled out from behind the rocks, startling the blue. It whinnied shrilly, reared up on hind legs, and almost rode him down as it shot away. Reins trailing, it went through the water and up the rise on the other side. There it stopped, watching them.

'Out cold,' Mayo informed the chuckling Charley Noonan as he came out from hiding, tossing aside the free end of the lariat. 'Hit his head when he fell. Bleeding some.'

'That's the least of his worries,' Noonan grinned. Then, abruptly businesslike: 'Get his hands and feet tied. I'm takin' no more chances with this son!'

Mayo hunkered down beside the unconscious Rourke, using the slack length of the rope to secure his limbs. When through, still perched on his haunches, he looked up at his chunky companion. 'You still haven't told me what you got in mind . . .'

Noonan grinned. 'Kortman wanted that place in ashes didn't he?'

'Yeah, but—'

'And isn't this the bastard that done for Dave?' Before Mayo could answer, Noonan said: 'So we kill two birds with one stone.' He cocked his head at Mayo who was slowly rising to full height. 'You brought the oil?'

Mayo nodded. 'Yeah, but it ain't much.' He swallowed. 'Charley – you ain't figuring on . . . ?' Suddenly his head was shaking. 'Hell, no! That's Injun! A bullet sure, but . . .' He swallowed again, with greater difficulty. 'That's why you didn't want to just plug him – why you wanted to use the rope . . .'

Noonan's face tightened, setting hard against Mayo. 'You forgettin' what he did to us? Forgettin' it was him who gunned Amherst? You want his death pinned on us?'

'No, but—'

'Then load him on to your nag, and quit wastin' time. This bastard's gonna cook, and I hope it's real slow!'

A distance away, from between the concealment of rocks, a slight figure watched them load Rourke up on to one of their horses, then head for the stream. On the opposite bank the big roan gave a malevolent snort, wheeled sharply and made distance.

Noonan was the first to dismount when they reached the cabin. Roughly he jerked Rourke's body from where it was strung across Mayo's saddle. Rourke hit the dirt hard, but made no sound. Mayo swung to the ground, looked at the body. 'Must've really taken a crack to be out that cold.'

'Get the oil,' Noonan growled, 'and bring his hat. Don't want to leave anything around that'll raise questions.' He went up to the cabin, opened the door, muttering a curse when discovering how dark it was inside.

Minutes later they had Rourke sprawled face down on the wooden floor, the rope removed from his arms and legs. 'Slosh that oil around the bottom of the walls,' Noonan directed, 'and be sure to get some over him. I wanna be sure he roasts good.'

'Hell, Charley – no!' Mayo complained. 'You said nothing about—'

'I'm saying it now!' Noonan snarled. Then, his gaze still on Mayo silhouetted in the doorway, he pointed to the whiskey bottle the smaller man clutched. 'What th' hell! That all you brought?'

'Damnit, Charley – you know I had to swipe it! It's all I could manage without bein' seen.'

Noonan muttered something indecipherable, waved a hand at the cabin's dark interior. 'All right don't just stand there! Get to it! Make sure there's enough to get the doors and windows going first. And don't forget – I want some on him!' He turned for the door, leaving Mayo to get on with the job.

There was less than half a cup left in the bottle when Mayo was done. In the middle of the floor Rourke was no more than a dark bundle. Mayo kicked the black hat he'd dropped beside the body still closer, started to tip the bottle, and stopped. Instead of following instructions, he emptied the bottle in front of the door leading to the cabin's second room.

By the time Mayo came out of the cabin, Howie Ballentine had moved in closer. The light was almost completely gone now and there wasn't much moon, but he had no trouble keeping track of their activity. He saw a match struck, the flame suspend itself in the air, and then what might have been a bit of grease-wood or creosote-bush flare larger and brighter. Their voices reached back to where he hid, but not loud enough to be understood.

Shortly afterwards he heard what sounded like a door closing, and then from inside the cabin came growing light as flames raced along the walls and crawled up to the windows. Mayo and Noonan, again mounted, were backed away, watching the brilliance intensify, listening as timber snapped and popped, until flames began licking through the wood shingled roof. Only when they appeared to be completely satisfied that no one could escape the inferno did they swing their horses about and ride away.

Howie remained, eyes bright, the smile on his small face growing as he watched flames eat away at the shack, until after just a short while there was nothing to be seen but a roaring blaze. Only then did he start back to where he'd left the chestnut.

He was softly whistling as he rode away, a lively Mexican tune the title of which he did not know. He owed Noonan and Mayo; they'd done what he'd been trying to do – only they'd done it in a way he'd not thought of. Yep . . . he owed them, and maybe he'd even pay off – eventually. Especially Charley Noonan who'd so often snickered behind his back.

For the moment, though, all that counted was the fact that Rourke was dead, and he was again safe.

But the instant Noonan had slammed the cabin door the subject of Howie's thoughts was moving. Consciousness had returned before they'd dropped him off Mayo's horse, but, knowing that from where he lay he had little chance of doing anything of value, he'd continued to play possum. Now as he pushed up on to his feet, instinctively reaching for his hat while watching the flames streak along the base of the wall, Rourke wasn't so sure it had been the smart thing to do. They'd made certain the fire would be the most intense at the doors and windows.

As the flames leapt higher, rapidly stretching towards the roof while still crawling across the floor, there was a brightness in the room that lit up everything. Thickening smoke and heat that was starting to make breathing difficult gave rise to a touch of panic. He could rush the door, perhaps succeed in shouldering it open – and walk right into their guns. He ditched the idea.

The one place in the cabin the flames had not yet

reached was the fireplace – probably because Mayo
had seen no point in wasting any of the coal oil there.
His gaze flitted to the wood-storage bin. Though
flames licked at its base, it remained relatively
untouched. He went to it, raised the lid, reached in
and flung out what was left of the wood. Climbing
inside was something of a struggle, but he managed,
pushing through to the other side of the box, holding his breath before shoving up against the outside
lid.

Cold air swept down upon him. He sucked it deep
into his lungs before pushing the lid all the way up.
He straightened slowly, and threw a leg over the
box's outer edge. Then, crouched low, headed for
the grove at the rear of the cabin.

From there he waited while flames began to poke
through the roof, eventually listening to it collapse, a
section at a time.

By morning there was only the stone chimney
standing forlornly at the end of the blackened and
smoking ruin, and not a living thing in sight. The
fire, he was certain, would have been seen by at least
one of the neighbouring homesteaders, yet none
had come to find out what it meant, or to render aid.
Was fear of retaliation from the Diamond B that
great? he wondered.

He was still thinking about it, still looking at what
was left of Kieffer's home when he heard the sound
of a horse. He stepped back into the protection of
the pines, waiting. The quiet thud of hoofs continued, drew closer, then halted. A soft, questioning
whinny travelled across the open space, as if the
animal was conscious of another presence.

Rourke came clear of the timber, and whistled.
Again the horse whinnied, this time louder, and

again there was the quiet thudding of shod hoofs.

Reins still trailing, head bobbing, the roan came up to greet its owner.

FOURTEEN

Scowling at his younger brother, Ballentine got up from the breakfast table. 'You're looking pretty damned smug this morning, considering the kind of problems you've got riding your back.'

Howie shrugged, pushed back his chair and also rose. 'What's to worry about?'

'Rourke, for starters. He knows you're the one he wants. He as much as told me so.'

Howie shrugged. 'He doesn't scare me. Not any more. Besides, there's nothing he can prove.'

'Different tune to the one you were singing the other night.' Ballentine's eyes narrowed coldly. 'What the hell've you gone and done now?'

'Not a thing,' Howie smiled. 'I swear – not a single, solitary thing. Just decided to play the cards as they fall.'

Alecia waited until he left the room before turning worried eyes up to her older brother. 'Jeff, do you think. . . ?'

'I don't know, Sis,' he answered seriously. 'He's a bit too cheerful for nothing to have happened. But this I do know: Rourke's on to him. How he tumbled to it, I don't know. But he knows Howie's the one he's looking for.'

Alecia stood up. 'And you're going to town – again?'

'Have to,' he said a little more tightly than intended. 'Want to be sure someone took the advice he was given. Maurie and Yarbrough will be riding with me.'

Howie waited, keeping himself out of the way while Kortman assigned duties to the crew, until he and Yarbrough rode off with Jeff. Only then did he saddle his own mount.

West of the Diamond, on a hill heavily crowned with brush, Jesse Vance and Burt Dwyer watched the activity in the ranch yard. Dwyer, right arm cradled in a crude sling, narrow face displaying his discomfort, said, 'Still say we take what we already been paid, get the hell out of here.'

'We're gettin' out OK, but only after we pick up a little extra change.' Vance moved his gaze from the now deserted yard. 'Big place that spread, ain't it?'

'Listen,' complained Dwyer, 'this arm's givin' me hell. I gotta see a sawbones.'

'Which's why we're cuttin'. No ways can we go into town an' have you patched up. Could be Rourke and that dame went to the law with our descriptions. Can't just sit here either, waitin' for Ballentine to come up with somethin' new.'

Dwyer snorted derisively. 'I still think he set us up. First the girl comes ridin' in, then the one we're supposed to've been paid to kill comes in shootin'! That the sort of place to send us to hole up?' He shook his head. 'It stinks!'

'Yeah, well . . . no use cryin' over it now. Maybe he didn't even expect anything like that.' Vance was quiet for a moment. 'Remember when Ballentine paid us, after tellin' us we had to clear out? He had to go back to the house, to that office of his, to get the money.'

'So?'

'So it's my guess he keeps a good stash on hand.'

'You're nuts!' Unconsciously Dwyer's fingers moved to the spare gun he'd borrowed from Vance 'Nobody with any sense would think of ridin' in there and—'

'Where the hell you been keepin' your eyes?' Vance cut in moodily. 'You just seen that young punk leave, and everybody else's already cleared off. At best there's no more'n the cook and the 'smith left. Them and the two women – that Mex housekeeper and the skinny sister.'

Alecia paid no attention to the sound of horses approaching; riders were always coming and going. Only when a knock sounded at the front door of the house did she consider the arrival of anyone other than Diamond riders.

'Yes. . . ?' she frowned when opening the door and finding Jesse Vance's pock-marked face smiling grimly at her.

'Mornin',' he greeted, small mouth twisted into a smile. 'Your brother handy?'

Alecia hesitated, a cold spot blossoming in her stomach. 'No . . . But he'll be back shortly. Is there something you wanted?' Her gaze moved beyond him, down to where Dwyer stood holding the reins of their horses in a hand projecting from a bandanna doubling as a sling. The holster tied down against his right leg was empty, but a gun stuck behind his belt was set for a left-hand draw.

'Matter of fact,' Vance nodded, holding the smile, 'there is.' He nodded to the far right of the veranda, to the closed door of Ballentine's office. 'You got a safe of some kind in there?'

Again Alecia hesitated.

Vance chuckled softly, and palmed his gun. 'How about you show it to us?'

Alecia stiffened. 'It would do you no good. Only my brother has the key.'

'Well, now' – Vance thumbed back the Colt's hammer – 'let's go find out if that's the truth you're telling.'

Rourke knew he was taking a chance. Confronting Ballentine on his home ground, especially after the threat made in the Phoenix, would be pushing his luck. At that time of morning, though, most of the hands would already be out on the range. Ballentine himself might not even be around. But if he was, it would be interesting to see his reaction to the charges about to be made.

Two horses stood in front of the house, a man holding their reins as if he were there waiting for someone. When Rourke stepped the roan into the yard, he spun quickly around, revealing an arm held across his front by a make-shift sling.

For Rourke there was no immediate identification, not until he saw the reins dropped and the man's unencumbered hand streak to the gun stuck behind his belt.

Rourke reined the blue to the right swinging himself from the saddle at the same moment that lead tore aside the tranquillity of the morning. His Colt was fisted and pointed when he hit ground. Another shot from the house went equally wild, succeeding only in driving the horses the man had held still further away.

Rourke fired.

Dwyer took a backward step, paused, then weaved forward. He'd not yet collapsed when Alecia Ballentine was shoved through the door of the room at the end of the veranda. A narrow-shouldered, wild-eyed man was using his left to hold on to both a small canvas bag and her left arm. His other hand jammed a gun into her side.

'Drop it!' he screamed. 'Drop it or she dies!' By then Rourke was almost at the veranda. Vance yelled again. 'I mean it, damnit!' Then, in an unconscious act of stupidity, as if hoping to emphasize his threat, he moved the gun from the girl's side, meaning to point it at her head. 'Throw down your gun or—'

Before he could finish, Alecia Ballentine screamed shrilly and performed a wild and risky act – something she herself would later have difficulty in understanding. In one tight and unexpected movement she jerked away from her captor, letting her knees unhinge the moment she was free of his grasp. She was still going down when Rourke put the bullet through Vance's chest.

The door at the front of the house opened. The Mexican woman came lumbering out, heavy brows arched high. Her eyes swept the veranda, saw Alecia trying to regain her feet; she raced to her, screaming frantically.

By then the cook and the blacksmith were in the yard, and what followed was a tangle of questions. Finally, Alecia came over to where Rourke waited.

'It appears,' she said somewhat stiffly, as if what was needed to be said presented some sort of personal embarrassment, 'I may well have to thank you for my life.'

Rourke shrugged. 'You know them?'

Alecia hesitated, but the cook spoke up readily. 'Yeah – the boss hired 'em. Only later he changed his mind an' paid 'em off.'

Rourke's glance shifted back to the girl.

She said, 'Jeff ... Jeff had a bad feeling about them. He ... decided it best to pay them a month's wages and let them go.' She took a deep breath. 'It appears he was right. They were here in an attempt to rob us.'

Rourke nodded, though he had a hunch he wasn't hearing all the truth. 'Your brother not around?'

'No,' she answered. 'He left for town. A while ago.'

'How about Noonan and Mayo?'

Remembering that he'd asked about Charley Noonan the first time he was at the ranch, Alecia's brow furrowed. 'What business would you have with them?'

'Nothing that can't wait,' he said, and jerked a thumb at where Dwyer was sprawled. 'Be an idea to get them into town, make a report to the sheriff.'

'I'll see that it's done,' she told him. And after a small hesitation. 'I thank you again, Mr Rourke.'

FIFTEEN

Billy Deacon was at the side of the old horse whose name he could not speak, when the sound of someone coming up along the access road brought his head sharply around. He stiffened, hastily trying to complete the task of tightening a badly worn cinch. Before he could do so, Howie Ballentine was already drawing in close.

'Got troubles, dummy?'

Billy made as if he'd not heard.

Howie drew his gun and fired a shot that cleared the oldster's head by scant inches. The old swayback tried to jerk free, but Billy held on, though almost pulled off his feet. A jumble of exasperated sounds rasped from his throat when he turned to glare at the youngest of the Ballentine litter.

'How's that?' Howie grinned. 'Can't hear you. Speak a little louder!' He fired again, this time nicking a piece from the shoulder of Billy's over-size coat. 'Now, what was that you were saying, Billy Boy?'

Billy's head swayed from left to right, as if hoping to find help or some method of escape.

Howie chuckled and hooked a leg around the pommel of his saddle, never once allowing the muzzle of the gun to stray from the old man and his horse. Once comfortable, he took his time, stretching his arm to its full extent squinting along the gun's barrel, drawing a bead on the space between Billy's eyes. His finger tightened around the trigger – tilting the barrel to the sky a fraction of a second before the hammer fell, laughing at the thin, strangled cry of fear coming from Billy's withered throat.

For Billy Deacon, the next fifteen minutes were an eternity in Hades, but for the boy it was like no time at all.

'That old crowbait you got there,' he said, pointing the gun at the horse. ' 'Bout time, don't you think, he was permanently retired? What say we use this bright and beautiful morning to send him off to horse heaven – or wherever the hell it is they go when they're done? What you say, old man? Think that a good idea?' The Colt levelled.

Still holding tightly to the reins, Billy sprang in front of the animal, arms protectively outstretched. His head shook desperately, the sounds scratching across his lips the closest he could manage to a plea.

'Well, then, how about you, Billy Boy? You ready to cash in? I mean, you're not a whole hell of a lot of use to anyone, now, are you? Why, man, I could take off both your ears and it'd—' He broke off sharply, seeing a sudden change in Billy Deacon's frightened expression. Forehead corrugating, he twisted in leather. Then he stared – stared hard – and the sound that ripped up from his gut was hardly different from anything Billy Deacon might have made.

'No!' he breathed. 'It – it's impossible!'

Sudden panic was a cable of steel tightening around Howie Ballentine's chest. He had to be seeing things! But that horse, he'd seen only one like it around Redemption! He'd also seen its rider consumed in flames!

The racket of distant gunfire, muffled by the hilly terrain, reached Rourke long before he spotted the two horsemen halted below clumps of scrub oak growing along the top of a ridge. Then a twist in the road removed them from view, and by the time he'd rounded the bend they were no longer in sight. One had appeared vaguely familiar, but the rider strad- dling the chestnut had been turned the wrong way.

He heard the cries a while before arriving at the spot where he'd seen them. Drawing rein, he glanced up at the ridge. This time it was more than just a cry that rose into the air, this time it was a stri- dent howl of pain. He turned the blue off the trail, urging it up the slope.

On the other side the land fell steeply down to a dry creek-bed, its banks thickly fringed with chapar- ral high enough to hide a man. He let his gaze sweep the area, almost immediately sighting the old sway- back standing in a small clearing. Touching heels to the blue, he cut a line down through the brush, aiming straight for the horse.

A few yards from where the animal was stationed he found Billy Deacon on his hands and knees, softly whimpering. Blood streamed down the side of his bare head. His battered hat lay close to the horse's front hoofs. Something hard had been laid viciously across the side of his skull.

Rourke swung down, thinking of nothing except that the old man was in trouble and needed help. Hardly had his boots found earth when from behind him came a shout:

'Freeze! That's right – throw them up – both of

them!' The voice was more than just a little shaky.

'Wondered where you'd crawled to,' Rourke said tightly, lifting his hands. He nodded toward Billy. 'You do that to him just to get me down here?'

'It worked, didn't it? Old Billy there sure can shout when he has to. Now shut up! Just stand still and shut up!' Cautious footsteps moved in closer. 'That's right! Keep it like that! One wrong move and I'll blow your spine apart.'

'Same's you did to Wally Hatton when you raided our camp?'

'Should've been you!' Howie snarled, reaching out quickly to whip the Colt from Rourke's holster. 'But we'll fix that.'

He circled wide around Rourke, small face twisted in hate. Lips flattened over small, perfectly straight teeth when he came to a halt. 'How the hell'd you get out of that fire?'

'That one of your ideas?'

'No, but I saw what happened – and I'm waiting to hear how you got away.'

Rourke shrugged. 'Magic.'

'That was a mistake, that night,' Howie said bitterly, knowing he'd get no more explanation. 'I should've used an extra bullet to make sure you were dead.' He paused, frowning. 'How'd you find out? You sure as hell didn't recognize me when you pitched up at the ranch. And damned if I recognized you without the beard. So how?'

'From something you left behind that night. Up until yesterday, though, I had trouble remembering what it was.'

Howie motioned impatiently with the gun. 'Left what?'

Rourke looked down at the boy's hand-tooled

boots, remembering the imprint Ellen's boot had made in the damp soil out at the JT. 'It was raining that night remember? The ground was soft – and you left behind a complete bootprint. The print of a small boot – smaller than most average men would wear. The kind that'd most likely belong to a light-weight half-pint.'

A snarl contorted Howie's mouth. 'Clever. But a lot of good it's going to do you. This's where you get what you should've got the first time!'

Behind the boy Billy Deacon was trying to get to his feet but the effort was too much. He uttered a quiet groan, and rolled over on to his side. Howie shot a fast glance his way. 'Shut up, you crazy old bugger!'

Rourke's gaze turned stony. 'A hotshot like you,' he said quietly, tone revealing what he felt for the boy, 'probably knows most of what goes on around here. Maybe even the name of the party who gunned down the owner of the JT.'

Howie's chuckle was thin and frigid. 'Ought to – seein' as it was me. We had use for his land, needed the water and the flats.'

Billy Deacon had succeeded in pushing himself up on to an elbow. His mouth moved soundlessly as he listened. Then, with a cry that was like nothing Rourke had ever heard before, the old man used everything he had left in a violent effort to thrust upwards and lurch in Howie Ballentine's direction.

Startled, Howie whirled, firing twice.

Rourke lunged forward as he was coming around, going in low and hard. Another shot exploded above his head, and then the boy was slamming into the ground, Rourke on top of him, fingers of his left hand gripped vice-like around a thin wrist.

It took barely any effort to overpower the youngest of the Ballentines. Rourke stood over him, looking at Billy Deacon's bleeding body from the corner of his eye. Mention of the JT had obviously meant something to him. Perhaps only its connection to Ellen Terry, the girl he considered a friend.

'Brave little polecat aren't you?' he muttered, eyes cold as grey mountain mist. 'Hope you're as brave when they get you ready to dance on air.'

Howie sat up, head shaking tremulously. 'Listen,' he whined. 'The old man he was nothing. Just a crazy old coot. But we – you and me we can work something out. The money I took from you – I'll give it back! Double!' Tears began trailing down his cheeks, his voice breaking into a series of blubbering sobs. 'More, even! Anything you want! We've got money. We can set you up—'

Rourke took a threatening forward step. 'Shut your snivelling mouth!' he said tightly. 'Shut it before I do it for you!'

SIXTEEN

It was going to be a bad day. Burrell had the feeling long before he crawled out of bed. Now, at his desk, the one-page special edition of the *Redemption Register* before him, he knew it for a certainty. He took a long pull at the freshly made coffee, felt it settle hot and sour in his stomach, and read the item again. Set in type larger than the newspaper normally used, it was positioned inside a heavy frame in the centre of the page where no one could miss it.

REWARD
$500

This week, Dave Amherst, at the time employed by the Diamond B, was murdered by a party still at large, in spite of strong circumstantial evidence pointing to the killer.

The law in Redemption, however, considers it insufficient to warrant an arrest.

Diamond B demands that justice be served upon Dave Amherst's murderer, and, therefore, offers a reward of $500 to anyone able to render assistance in bringing this about.

J. BALLENTINE

The rest of the page was filled with bits about how Jake Ballentine had established the Diamond B, how he had founded the town of Redemption, and fought for county status. Burrell flung the paper aside. Though not once was Rourke's name mentioned, there could be little doubt that Ballentine had arranged for it to be spread around the saloons. The thing amounted to little more than an invitation for anyone so inclined to go bounty-hunting. He took another swig of the coffee, then retrieved the paper from the floor. He'd need to have a few tough words with the *Register*'s publisher. Not that he expected it to produce much good. Vivien Noldoff had always been, and would probably always be, a boot-licking supporter of the Ballentine clan.

Looking down Redemption's broad main street Tom Harding felt oddly disoriented. When, early that morning, he'd left the ranch he knew exactly what he was going to do, but now that he was here things were no longer quite so clear. He shook his head, as if to shake his thoughts back into rational order, but all it achieved was to send sharp pain streaking dead-centre through his skull. He'd had something he wanted to tell Rourke about Howie Ballentine, and he'd known exactly how to handle it. But sometime during the ride it occurred to him that the time wasn't yet right. Trouble now, especially shooting trouble, could delay the wedding. Even put an end to it. Besides, the man appeared not to be in town.

He wanted also to see Doc Sturrett, that he knew. He'd seldom suffered from headaches, but recently they'd been arriving with increased frequency. He paused on the sidewalk, realizing that Kate's Kitchen was right across the street, and that he'd not had much of a breakfast. Hardly had the thought registered when he was in motion, the call on the medico forgotten.

Further down the street, Frank Burrell left the newspaper office and stopped to watch the owner of Rafter H when he came out of the Phoenix. It had him curious, for Harding visited town only when absolutely necessary. The ridges in the sheriff's forehead deepened as he observed the abrupt crossing to the café. Something didn't seem altogether right.

There were only two other customers in the café, sitting at separate tables. Harding ignored both, heading directly to the far corner of the room where he'd have a view on to the street.

One of the late morning diners was a chunky man with several days' mottled growth bristling around his lower face. His name was Phil Calley, and he was feeling like five kinds of hell. Most of his condition could be credited to the fact that he'd been drinking ever since hitting town; the rest to the memory of how close he'd recently come to having his life snuffed out.

He was still foggy on that score, remembering only being run out of the saloon – being shoved through the door, hearing a shot as he went sprawling across and over the edge of the sidewalk. He remembered nothing of scrambling up from the dirt, somehow stumbling away. He wasn't even sure when or where he'd heard about the deputy being killed.

Nor when he remembered whom he'd seen step briefly from the darkened mouth of an alley, level his gun once more – then, without firing, quickly turn and run. It took a while for it to dawn on him that he was probably the only one who'd had so much as a glimpse of the gunman.

After Burrell had got his name from the Phoenix's barkeep and hauled him in for questioning, he'd almost blurted out everything he remembered. But for reasons then not understood, he'd clammed up, and in doing so an even better idea was born. If used the smart way, what he had could be turned into big money, more than enough to get the hell and gone from here, someplace where he could take it easy.

First, though, he needed to properly sober up, get himself in better shape, so that when he put forward his proposition they'd know he was someone to be reckoned with.

The task, though, was not proving easy.

Through bloodshot eyes he studied the new arrival, blinking several times in an attempt to sharpen his focus. He took another swig of the cold coffee he was nursing, and felt his stomach lurch.

He badly needed a drink – several drinks to still the shaking in his gut, the trembling of his hands. But he was broke – had been for a while, ever since losing his job at Rafter H.

'Well, now,' he heard a slurred voice say, 'if it ain't Mr High and Mighty hisself!'

Tom Harding looked up, ruddy face clouding dangerously. 'Thought you'd have enough sense to realize you're washed up around here.'

'Yeah,' Calley snarled, lowering the coffee-cup. 'Fixed it so's nobody else'd hire me, didn't you?'

'Calley,' Harding said, struggling to keep the anger out of his voice, feeling the pain in his skull gouge deeper, 'get out of here! You're making me sick!'

Calley scraped back his chair. '*You* gonna make me?'

'Get out!' Harding repeated. 'You're drunk and you stink!'

In the process of pushing to his feet, Calley was forced into a tottering backward step. Clumsily he righted himself, left hand grabbing at the table for support, almost overturning it.

'Gentlemen – *please*!' Kate Charlton, the chubby middle-aged proprietor, shouted. 'Take your argument outside!'

But Phil Calley heard nothing. Vaguely he was aware of the other customer going through the open door, but his eyes were only for Tom Harding, now almost vertical, pulling back his coat to get at his gun. Calley made a clumsy snatch for his holstered Remington, had it clear when lead smashed into the wall behind him. In his shaking hand his own gun bucked twice.

Kate Charlton screamed, cupped hands leaping to her mouth when she saw the pistol in Tom Harding's hand start to droop, the colour drain from his face. His free hand pressed against his middle, blood trickling slowly through old, rope-scarred fingers. 'No,' he groaned painfully. 'No ... not now ... not now. . . .'

Calley, stared, swallowed – tried to say something and felt bile instead of words rise up in his throat. His gaze swung to the open street-door.

Frank Burrell was almost at the café when, moments after hearing the shots and the woman's scream, he saw Calley come lunging on to the street.

'Hold it!' he bellowed.

Calley skidded to a stop, twisting in the direction of the voice, the old Remington still gripped in his fist. Almost stupidly he stared at it, then lifted his eyes back to where the sheriff stood.

Burrell saw the gun shift, the indecision in the puncher's face, but chose not to gamble. He fired, saw Phil Calley take three staggering backward steps while still clinging to the gun. The fat lawman's second shot brought him down.

Among those who came to see what was going on were Ballentine, Yarbrough and Kortman. Burrell ordered a couple of men to get the bodies moved to the undertaker, then turned to Ballentine, who appeared hardly perturbed by what had happened.

'You want to take the news to Spense?'

Ballentine shrugged. 'You go, Ben,' he instructed Yarbrough. 'Better get word to Alecia, too.'

'Be able to tell her yourself,' Maurie Kortman murmured, squinting along the street. 'Less'n I'm seein' things, that's her on the buckboard, and Gatlin's doin' the drivin'.'

'Now what the blazes,' Ballentine muttered, straightening up, 'is she here for?'

Instead of answering, Burrell stepped out into the middle of the street to intercept them.

A while later, in the sheriff's office, after Alecia had told her story of the foiled robbery attempt by Vance and Dwyer, Burrell said, 'Strikes me you got something to thank Rourke for, Jeff.' From his desk he picked up the special edition of the *Register*, and tossed it to Ballentine. 'Maybe enough to do something about this before things get out of hand.'

Ballentine threw the paper back on the desk. 'It stands.'

'Your decision,' Burrell sighed. 'Just one thing I'd like to know. What made you send for those two? Haven't yet checked, but it would surprise me none if in one of these drawers I don't find dodgers for them both.'

'It was a mistake,' Ballentine grunted. 'Only when they got here did I find out what they were like. So I got rid of them – like I told you.' He moved to where Alecia was seated. 'Come on, Sis, I'll take you home.' Then he turned to Kortman leaning up close to the door. 'You might's well come back as well. Yarbrough can stick around a while.'

Howie Ballentine sat morosely atop the chestnut, hands firmly secured, his gun where it would do no more damage. A few feet away, nervously pawing the earth, Billy Deacon's horse waited, a roped bundle slung across its battered saddle.

'You'll never make it to town,' he sneered. 'Jeff's probably already on his way back to the ranch – with two of our men. We'll run into them, and when we do, you're dead meat!'

'Should it happen,' Rourke said. 'They'll be digging a hole for you before the day's done.'

Getting the boy back to town without interference was a problem Rourke had been chewing on. The Ballentines were a power, and they'd have many allies in people anxious for the family's favour.

SEVENTEEN

It was the longer and slower way back to town, but Rourke chose to stay off the wagon road, not wanting to encounter anyone at this stage. Especially not Jeff Ballentine or any of his crew.

In the early afternoon hours Redemption was quiet, with not many on the street and sidewalks. But beneath the surface of serenity Rourke sensed tension – as if the town was waiting for something to happen. Or as if something already had. The few who stopped to watch him come down the wide street, with Howie Ballentine riding at his side, appeared not to notice the boy's hands tied to the saddle horn. Most interest was focused on the old led horse and its tarp-wrapped bundle.

A tall redhead stepped to the edge of the walk, gazing hard at the man upon the blue roan. One of many who'd read the special one-shot edition of the town's paper, his hand caressed the gun riding his thigh, but from there it moved no further. What the hell, he puzzled, was young Ballentine doing in the company of the one they said had killed the Diamond rider?

By the time Rourke was tying up at the rack in front of the law office, two others had joined the redhead.

His mind a tangle of thoughts, Burrell sat at his desk, puffing on a cigar, staring at the blank wall on the other end of the room. When the street door opened, letting in Howie Ballentine, with Rourke close at his back, he took a last pull on the thin black weed before depositing it in the ash-tray. He said nothing. And if the appearance of the two held any surprise, he kept it concealed.

Rourke shut the door behind him, nudging the boy further into the office. 'Found Ken Tobin,' he said, dropping Howie's gun on the desk.

Howie, his face like a small piece of parchment stubby nose pinched tight held up his bound wrists. 'You know what's good for you, Frank, you'll get this rope off me, *pronto*!'

Slowly, Burrell lifted his bulk from the old swivel chair. He eyed Rourke. 'You were saying?'

'He's the one killed my partner – shot and robbed me. The one that killed the girl, and the storekeeper up in Astoria. He's also bragged about killing the owner of the JT.'

Burrell's small eyes became granite chips. 'It was you who killed Jack Terry?'

'He's lying!' Howie shouted. 'Damn you, Burrell – you listen to him you're in for big trouble.' Again he raised his roped wrists. 'Now get me untied, damnit!'

'Outside,' Rourke went on, 'you'll find the body of Billy Deacon. This bit of chicken dung put two bullets into him – while the old man was unarmed and down on the ground.'

Burrell's sharp glare cut short Howie's next outburst. 'You two wait here,' he ordered, and left the office.

'You're going to regret this!' Howie breathed venomously. 'Nobody does this to me and gets away with it. When my brother gets here he'll carve out your guts!'

Rourke gave him no response, listening instead to the voices out on the sidewalk, to Burrell giving directions to someone.

Returning to the office, Burrell resumed his position behind the desk. He looked at the boy. 'You've done it this time, kid. This's not the kind of fix I can pull you out of.'

'What fix?' Howie demanded loudly. 'You going to listen to all his lies? How about listening to me – and getting these damn ropes loose?'

Burrell ignored him, picked up the gun Rourke had handed in, and checked the chambers. 'Two rounds fired,' he muttered, closing the gate, depositing the weapon back on the desk, a little off to the left. 'Must've reloaded, if it was him firing those shots you say you heard.'

'He's lying, damnit!' Howie yelled furiously. 'Who you going to believe, Burrell? Him or me?'

Burrell gave him a cold, pitying scrutiny. 'Outside there's a body waiting for the undertaker to fetch. Want to explain that?'

'I don't have to explain nothing! He was hauling it along when I ran into him. Ask him why he killed the old coot!'

Burrell's sigh came from down deep as he took Howie's arm. 'Come along, boy.'

'No!' Howie hissed. 'You're not locking me up!' He tried to pull away, but Burrell's hand was a clamp around his upper arm. 'Damn you, Frank – let me go!'

While Howie was led to the cells, over in the Phoenix, appearing even more perplexed than usual, Spense Harding had his elbows propped on the bar, oblivious to the sounds and movements

around him. He was still finding it hard to accept
that his father was dead – harder still to believe how
it had happened. About to call for another drink, he
came slowly around when the batwings flew open
and boots stomped heavily across the floor.

'Heard the news?' a voice boomed. The man who
had just entered waited until he had everyone's
attention before continuing. 'That Rourke feller
everyone's been talkin' about, he just brought in ol'
Billy Deacon's body. And get this – he's also hauled
in Howie Ballentine. Claims he seen him gun down
the old codger!'

Seated alone at a table, Ben Yarbrough's big hand
tightened around his glass. He listened to the questions being fired at the news-bearer, then, realizing
the man knew no more than he'd already told,
finished his drink and started for the street.

By then Spense Harding had already left, arriving
at the sheriff's office only seconds before Yarbrough.

'Young Harding's taking his father's death pretty
bad. Along with this business, it'll likely put a crimp
in his wedding plans,' Burrell said quietly.

Rourke had no opinion on the matter, so said
nothing.

Dusk was already falling, but both men were still in
the sheriff's office.

For a while Burrell was silent. Then he asked:
'That business out at the ranch – Vance and Dwyer
trying to rob the Ballentines. It happen like Miss
Alecia told it to me?'

'Pretty much.' So far he'd said nothing about what
had happened at the Kieffer cabin. It was something
that would hold.

The sheriff shifted uneasily in the old swivel chair.

'Shouldn't be too long before Ballentine gets here. Yarbrough's had more than enough time to get the news to him.'

'Figure on trouble?'

'For a certainty. He won't stand still knowing his kid brother's been locked up. Probably bring most of his crew with him when he comes.' Hands laced themselves across his belly while his gaze moved from where he'd placed Howie's gun to Rourke's face. 'No reason for you to stick around. Keeping the kid in custody's my responsibility. You've sworn out a complaint, done all that's required of—'

The office door opening unexpectedly gave him no chance to finish. Both he and Rourke got out of their chairs when the door shut behind a redheaded number who was followed in by two shorter men. He gave Rourke a cautious glance. The hands of all three were hung close to their guns.

'Ain't this the one Jeff Ballentine's offerin' a reward for?' the sorrel-head asked.

The sheriff's face set hard in a mixture of disdain and anger. But when he spoke his voice was calm. 'The man's name is Rourke,' he said. 'And I know nothing about any reward posted for him.'

'Knock it off, Sheriff. It's in that there paper on your desk,' one of the men behind the redhead sneered. 'You know what we're talkin' about.'

'What's the deal, Burrell?' the third man queried. Intendin' to collect the bounty yourself?'

While they spoke Burrell had picked up the paper, scanning the page again. He glanced up, frowning. 'You boys are getting me a tad confused – and more than just a little bit riled. This man came in here voluntarily, and he's free to leave any time he wants. I got nothing on him. As for Ballentine offering a reward for anyone of his name or description' – he flung the paper at the redhead – 'show me where it says anything like that!'

The redhead blinked, suddenly uncertain of his ground. Before he could open his mouth Burrell's voice was lashing at him. 'Now let me tell you hotshots something. Right after that thing came out I sent a copy to the Federal Marshal's office, along with a letter explaining a few things. So now I'm giving you boys fair warning; you let that notice tempt you to do something stupid it'll be on your own heads. You'll have nobody but your fool selves to blame when they fit you with hemp neckties.'

For the first time that day Burrell permitted himself a small smile. 'Then again, if you *hombres* are real determined, I won't stand in your way.' Abruptly he dropped the smile. 'But I'll be on hand to get whichever one of you he might miss killing.'

For a long breath no one spoke. Burrell's voice again broke the silence. 'Now, you got any sense, you'll get out of here, fast and you'll spread the word to other hotheads like yourselves!'

When the door closed behind them, Rourke said, 'What if they'd tried something?'

Burrell snorted scornfully. 'They didn't. Still, you'd best watch your back. Could be other idiots like them out there.'

Rourke frowned. 'You write that letter?'

'Hell, no! Had too much else on my mind to think about it. But they don't know that.' Burrell flopped heavily into his chair, picked up a half-smoked cigar from the glass tray, and wedged it between his lips. 'Now, not that I got a dislike for your company, but I think it best you're not here when the Diamond rides in.'

Rourke gave it a moment's thought, then shrugged. 'Guess I can understand that. But you want me – or they want me – I'll be over in the Phoenix.'

'I'll keep it in mind.' Burrell nodded, any humour that had been in him gone.

Rourke left the office and, though hungry, ignored his stomach's demands, and steered a course directly to the saloon.

At least thirty minutes had marched to their death since Rourke entered the Phoenix. All the while he'd been dawdling over a beer, conscious of the unnaturally quiet conversation for a Friday night. Aware also that the gangling redhead and his companions were sitting long-faced at one of the side tables. They'd seen him enter, but after that they kept their eyes to themselves, tossing occasional glances his way only when they thought he wasn't watching.

Word of the arrest had obviously got around, and like Burrell, few there believed Jeff Ballentine would take the jailing of his kid brother quietly. All waited for the explosion that was bound to come, and the covert glances he picked up in the back bar mirror told of their prime expectancy.

Most there waited to witness his fate. Because as sure as God would make the morrow, this night the man named Rourke would die under the guns of the Diamond.

He plucked the Durham sack from his pocket, was rolling a smoke, when, above the subdued noises of the saloon, his ears picked up the distant *rataplan* of hoofbeats.

EIGHTEEN

Behind him, Frank Burrell closed the door leading to the cells and guided the boy up to the side of his desk.

'What's going on now?' Howie Ballentine demanded. Then he cocked his head to the window, listened – and laughed harshly. 'So that's it! Jeff's bringing in the crew and you're backing down! You're letting me go.'

Burrell opened a drawer in the desk. 'Can't do that, boy. Only figured to let him see you here rather than in the cell. First, though, we got to put on these bracelets.'

'Think again!' Howie snarled, grabbing up his gun from where it still lay on the desktop, swiping the barrel hard across Burrell's knuckles.

The handcuffs fell to the floor and Burrell went back a step. 'Put it down, Howie! You're already in enough trouble.'

'Yeah? How much's enough?' His laugh turned thin, a little crazy. 'You already got enough to hang me.'

'Then Rourke was right. It was you who killed his

partner, and all the others. That girl – and Jack Terry.'

'And I'll kill you just as easy! So sit down, fat man!' He gave Burrell a hard shove, forcing him back into the swivel chair. 'I said sit down!'

He was backing to the door when Burrell said, 'That's as far as you go!' and brought up his hand from across his round middle.

Howie saw the gun lifting, pointing his way, and he fired. The first shot slapped high into the sheriff's shoulder, rocking him back into the chair, sending it sliding a few inches across the floor. The second found a spot a few inches lower.

Then Burrell fired. Just once.

The riders pulled up in front of the office, Jeff Ballentine and Maurie Kortman the first to leave their saddles. Ballentine opened the door, pushed, found it come up against an obstruction, and swore. He put his shoulder to the wood and heaved. The door flew open under his weight and he stormed in, almost tripping over the body that lay on its back, eyes and mouth stretched wide in shock, blood still spreading across its narrow chest.

Kortman came in after him, followed by Ben Yarbrough. They stopped sharply, watching him get down beside Howie's body. Neither could see what he did, nor hear what it was he mumbled. Slowly he rose and turned to where Frank Burrell was flopped in his chair, blood leaking from two wounds high in the left of his heavy body. He strode up to the desk, gun drawn.

'Tell me! Tell me, damnit!'

Burrell lifted pained eyes. 'Got him out so's you could talk in here. Was going to put the cuffs on him when he made a break – grabbed his gun and shot me.' A sigh hissed wearily. 'Had no option but to stop him.'

'You're lying!' Ballentine grated. 'How'd he get a gun, unless you rigged it so?' His own weapon lifted. 'Damn you, Burrell! You staged it – it was planned to happen like this!'

'That's a heck of an accusation, Jeff,' Burrell replied, voice starting to grow hoarse. 'But let's say you're right – say I figured I owed you something. Like this, it'll save your family a whole lot of embarrassment. This way none of the dirt gets to be heard in court.'

'Dirt?' Ballentine snarled, the front of his legs pressing hard against the old desk. 'What dirt?'

'The boy was a killer, Jeff. He killed all those Rourke told us about – killed old Billy Deacon in cold blood, and long ago he back-shot Jack Terry. Maybe there's even more we don't know about.' Burrell shook his head, slowly, somewhat sadly. 'I'm sorry for you, Jeff. You and Alecia. But I've an idea you already knew what I just told you.'

'You lie, you fat bastard! Howie killed nobody! You lie just like that son-of-a-bitch Rourke's been lying! It was him that started everything! Him that should be lying there dead. Not Howie! Not my brother! You sold us out, you yellow dog!' The gun in his hand bucked and belched, once, twice – a third time, and might well have emptied itself had Kortman not stepped in.

'That's enough, feller! More than enough!'

With a mighty sweep of his arm Ballentine knocked the tall ramrod aside, elbowed Yarbrough out of the way and strode heavily out on to the sidewalk.

Four men still sat their mounts. Two were hands

who'd been a long time at the Diamond. Les Mayo
and a grim-faced Charley Noonan made up the rest.
Both had heard of Rourke being in Redemption, and
both were still trying to digest the news. It would have
been impossible for him to escape the fire in that
cabin . . . yet somehow he had.

'You men listen,' Ballentine roared. 'My kid
brother's just been murdered. He's dead because of
something cooked up between the sheriff and the
man we know as Rourke. Burrell's already paid for
his part in it, but Rourke's still somewhere out there.
The man that brings him to me – alive or dead – will
get a thousand silver dollars!'

Charley Noonan turned to Mayo, and a smile
wiped the grimness from his face.

While they spoke, a spring wagon driven by Alecia
Ballentine rolled into town, stopping in front of the
hotel. She was dismounting when Spense Harding
who'd been watching the activity at the sheriff's
office stepped up to take her arm.

'Alecia, you shouldn't be here!'

'I heard Howie'd been arrested,' she said. 'I had to
come.' She turned her face up to his, clutching at his
arms, 'Spense what on earth is going on?'

Harding put an arm around her shoulders. 'I
think it best you come inside. I've a feeling that in a
little while a lot of lead is going to be flying.'

Everyone in the Phoenix had heard the shooting,
but so far none had moved. Rourke pushed away
from the bar, but he'd taken only three steps to the
door when the redhead and his companions were on
their feet, guns drawn.

'Stand pat!' the redhead shouted. 'That's
Diamond B out there, and they want you!'

Rourke turned slowly. 'Sonny, you going to use

that thing, do it fast. I'm walking out of here, and you try to stop me the undertaker'll be getting himself some extra business.'

One of the shorter men sneered, 'Big deal!' and fired. But he'd waited too long, permitting his eyes to betray his intention, and by then his target had moved. Rourke's shot smashed the would-be gunman's collar bone.

The redhead fired, and was also too slow. The shot that dropped him cut cleanly through his thigh. The third man threw away his weapon, grabbed sky and yelled, 'I'm out! I've quit!'

Rourke turned to the rest in the saloon. 'Anyone figuring on taking up where they left off?'

Hardly had he spoken when the batwings moved. Les Mayo poked his head inside, froze, then leaped backward, yelling: 'Charley! Charley! He's in here! He's in here!'

Rourke moved rapidly to the door, knowing he'd have to find time to reload. There were four shells left in his Colt and outside waited at least a half-dozen guns.

He pushed through the swing doors, leaping to the left of the entrance, in time to see Mayo charging across the street. As if sensing what was at his back, Mayo turned – saw Rourke, gave a startled yell, and fired in panic.

A single shot from left of the saloon doors ploughed into his chest. Mayo was still falling when, from the shadows crowding the opposite sidewalk, another voice sent up a loud curse. Muzzle-fire blossomed and Rourke felt lead burn along his ribs, knock him sideways at the same time a second shot furrowed through his coat and across his shoulder. He dropped to the boards, held his fire.

Along the street there was an abrupt cessation of activity. Rourke used the break to start punching out the spent cartridges. He managed only one before Charley Noonan's laugh shattered the temporary peace. 'I got him!' he yelled jubilantly. 'I got him!' He stepped out of the gloom, still laughing. 'Tell Ballentine I got the lousy—'

Near to the saloon's entrance he saw a shape suddenly rise. He tried to swallow and almost choked. The gun in his hand came up spitting, but he was too rattled for any of his shots to do much harm. Almost as if paralysed, Charley Noonan waited for the twin red and yellow flares from the front of the saloon, until lead hammered into his broad chest, knocking him backwards, and hard up against the wall at his rear.

Close to where Noonan had fallen voices were raised urgently. Above them all sounded that of Jeff Ballentine:

'Kill him! You hear me? *Kill him*! Two thousand to the man who brings me his head!'

A voice which, to where Rourke was backed into the shadows, sounded like that of Maurie Kortman, said, 'Jeff, stop! It's already gone too far!'

'What? What was that you said?' Rourke heard Ballentine's question thunder down the street, followed immediately by a blast of gunfire. He thought he heard someone utter a grunt of agony, but he couldn't be sure.

He came out to the edge of the sidewalk, still having had insufficient time to reload, knowing only one live cartridge was left in the cylinder of his Colt.

'Ballentine!' he shouted. 'It's over! Let it rest before more men die!'

From somewhere unseen the voice of Dr James Sturrett bellowed, 'He's right Ballentine! Your action has already cost too many lives! You're using this man as a scapegoat, and it won't—'

Ballentine's shot scraped past Rourke's head. His second shot went too wide. Rourke held his fire until the last moment and when he fired it was at the moment Ballentine chose to take two running steps further into the street. In reflex he squeezed trigger again, and heard the hammer come down on an empty cartridge.

Ballentine must also have realized his opponent had emptied his gun, for with a cry of triumph he stepped fully into view. 'Now I've got you!' he bellowed. 'Here's where you—'

'Jeff!' a voice called weakly. 'Jeff – enough is enough!'

Ballentine wheeled about, found Maurie Kortman standing, gun levelled at him. 'Maurie,' he breathed. 'What the hell. . . !'

'Howie was no good,' the Diamond foreman told him, the words coming haltingly. 'He never was. He was just plain no. . . .' Kortman never finished for Ballentine was cursing viciously, triggering his gun as he spat out the words.

But, though reeling, feeling the curtain of darkness already descending, some force within Maurie Kortman kept him vertical, kept Ballentine in clear view. With one final effort the man who had ramrodded the Diamond for so long clamped his finger around the trigger of his gun, keeping it rigid even after he was dead.

Jeff Ballentine had no sensation of the slugs ripping into him, no feeling of anything. The only thing he know as his legs folded, was confusion and astonishment. How in blazes could anyone so loyal as Kortman do a thing like this. . . ?

Over at the hotel, Alecia had insisted that Spense take her outside so that she might see for herself what was happening. Standing there now, she watched her oldest brother go down into the dirt of the street. She heeled sharply, burying her face into Harding's chest, an agonized cry wrenching itself from her heart. Spense's arm tightened around her thin shoulders, and at that moment, perhaps for the very first time, he realized how much he really cared for Alecia Ballentine.

Yet, even while watching men move toward the fallen, he was thinking of his father. *This is how you wanted it, wasn't it, Pa? It's all come to pass. Pretty soon the entire county will respond to the Harding name . . . and you'll never see it.*

The next morning, hat held against his leg, Rourke stood at the front door of the house on Coronado Street searching for words. And Ellen Terry, gazing up into his sun-scorched face, had never looked more radiantly beautiful than she did just then.

'I – I guess that's about it,' he said. 'Just . . . wanted to say goodbye.'

'You're leaving. . . ?' A little of her glow faded and a shadow flitted swiftly across the back of her eyes.

He shrugged awkwardly. 'Couldn't hang around, not after last night. But I couldn't leave without telling you goodbye.'

'Jay,' she said softly, 'Dr Sturrett told me everything that happened. He also told me of your part in it.' Her blonde head shook gently. 'You weren't to blame. It wasn't your fault!'

'Just the same, I . . .' He broke off, trying to avoid her eyes and the mist he saw rising in them. 'Ellen, I know I've got no right saying this, but – well, if I didn't, later on I'd regret it. And regrets I got enough of.'

She waited, hands clasped anxiously.

'Figured on riding up to Wyoming,' he said. 'Maybe there's still some chance of getting that spread me and Wally were after.'

'You will, Jay – you will.'

'Have to see about that. Still short on cash, and it might take some time.' He shifted his feet, using both hands to hold on to his hat. 'But, supposing, you're right. Do you think . . .' his grip on the hat tightened fiercely. 'Do you think you might like to – to look it over some time?'

'I can't think of anything I'd like more,' she said. 'I – I've already talked to Dr Sturrett about selling up here . . .'

'And if you two had any sense at all,' a voice boomed from somewhere not too far behind Ellen, 'you'd realize that together you already have more than you need to make a really good start.'

Rourke glanced quickly at the street. Until then he'd been too preoccupied with his own thoughts to have given the doctor's buggy more than passing attention. Turning back to Ellen he started a protest, but a small, soft and silencing hand placed itself over his mouth. 'Doc's right. We already have everything.' Quickly she stepped back, colour richly painting her cheeks. 'I mean if that's what . . .'

Rourke let his hat fall, and drew her into his arms. 'It's exactly what I meant. And if I never have a nickel, having you would be more than any man could ever want.'

'Now that,' a deep voice chuckled, 'is showing good sense!'